Bitter
Sweet

Jewelze T. Real

www.JohnsonPublicationsBooks.com

This book is a work of fiction. Names, characters, places and incidents either are products of the author's imagination or are used fictitiously. Any resemblance to actual events or locales or persons, living or deceased, is entirely coincidental.

ISBN 978-0-98-404166-4
Published by: Johnson Publications
Newtown Square PA
Copyright© 2012 by Jewelze and T. Real

Cover Layout/Design by Designs by SheShe
Editors: Carla Dean

Printed in the United States of America

Dedication

This book is dedicated to all of our loyal readers.
We love and appreciate you all!

Thank You

Thanks to all of those that continue to support our writing journey.

Bitter

Sweet

Corporate

Vixen

Jewelze

Rude Awakening

It was a beautiful spring afternoon. The sun shined brightly, warming the breeze that gently caressed everything it touched. Jaycee got out of classes early and decided to surprise Rick at his condo down by the waterfront. When she arrived, she realized the door of his condo was unlocked. She tiptoed in. Everything was quiet. Looking around, she noticed there were dirty dishes and empty Hennessey and Cristal bottles lying everywhere. It looked like Rick had a party and she hadn't been invited, which annoyed her.

"Sloppy muthafucka," she mumbled with an attitude.

An eerie feeling came over Jaycee as she continued inspecting the rooms for anything that might have appeared unusual. She slowly turned towards Rick's bedroom door, and something in the middle of the hallway floor caught her eye. She moved in for a closer look. Jaycee's heart raced when she discovered it was a woman's bra. After years of rumors and intuitions, she was about to be confronted with the ugly truth that awaited her behind the closed door of Rick's bedroom, which was less than ten feet away.

Jaycee quietly put down her school bag and slowly moved toward the door. She heard the faint sounds of pleasure coming from her man's bedroom. She knew it wasn't her making those sounds because she was standing on the other side of the door. Fear, anger, and hurt began to brew inside her. In an instant, she busted through the door like the police, only to find Rick in the middle of a pussy sandwich with two bitches who hung out at the bar where he conducted his underground business. There he was lying on his back with one chick sitting on his face and the other riding him. Jaycee went off, crying and cussing at the top of her lungs.

"You muthafucka! I knew you were dirty! How you gonna step out on me with these bitches?"

In a fit of rage, Jaycee rushed into the walk-in closet and grabbed the Louisville Slugger that Rick kept on a shelf along with a couple of Tech Nines, a Desert Eagle, and a sawed-off shotgun. Her first thought was to grab one of the guns and put a hole in his temple, but the reality of being behind bars for killing a low-life, son-of-a-bitch like Rick was not at the top of her priorities list.

Without thought, she grabbed the Louisville Slugger and commenced to swinging.

"Oh shit! Jaycee! What the fuck!" Rick yelled.

The girls screamed and tried to run for cover, but it was too late. Before one of the girls could get out of the bed, Jaycee surprised her with a blow to the back, which caused her to fall into the chaise lounge located in the corner of the room by the bed. The other tried to sneak out of the room while Jaycee delivered a few more shots to the girl's body as she curled up in a fetal position. Much to her dismay, she wasn't fast enough, and Jaycee surprised her with a hard blow to the side of her head, stretching her out in the middle of the floor.

Jaycee continued on her tirade, breaking up everything in her sight. She swung the bat about five good times, hitting Rick in the chest, arm, and stomach at least three of those five times.

"Awww fuck! Jaycee! What you doin'? What's wrong with you, girl?" Rick yelled in shock.

Jaycee continued swinging wildly. During his bitch-ass ducking to avoid getting clocked, he shouted for Jaycee to stop. Rick made one last attempt to spare himself from his fate with the bat.

"You should know them bitches don't mean shit to me! I love you, man! Come on! Stop swinging that fuckin' bat!"

Jaycee found it ironic that men always claimed the other bitches didn't mean anything and seemed to profess their undying love to their women when they were about to get fucked up!

As Jaycee reached back to swing the bat, she suddenly felt an excruciating pain radiate across her abdomen. She dropped the bat and fell to her knees, while Rick looked at her with concern.

"Jay, what's wrong? Yo, Jay...Jay!"

Jaycee tried to answer, but she couldn't because the pain was much too great. As she ran her hands across her pants, she realized they were wet. She looked down and screamed. Blood saturated her white Capri pants as she cried hysterically.

Rick ran to her side, looked down, and noticed her blood-stained pants.

"Oh shit! You're bleedin'! I gotta get you to the hospital!"

Jaycee rolled around on the floor in a ball, crying and screaming, "My baby! My baby! Oh God, please don't take my baby from me!"

Rick ran and grabbed his cell phone that sat on the nightstand by his king-sized bed to call the ambulance. For the first time in his life, fear rattled his voice as he yelled for the operator to dispatch an emergency medical unit immediately. Although all three women needed medical attention, he was only concerned about Jaycee, the mother of his unborn child.

After Rick hung up the phone, Jaycee felt something about the size of a grapefruit ooze out of her. Fear pierced her heart. At that moment, Jaycee felt a sense of emptiness. She knew then that the life she had grown to love over the past four and a half months was gone. She cried so hard that she passed out before the ambulance arrived.

* * * * *

As Jaycee laid in the hospital bed, doctors came in and out of her room, poking and prodding for what seemed like an eternity. She had to undergo a medical procedure called a D&C to make sure all evidence of her pregnancy had been extracted after the miscarriage. She looked out of the hospital window with red swollen eyes as she grieved about the events that had brought her to a place of turmoil. She felt no physical pain due to the painkillers, but they didn't kill the emotional pain that flowed through her heart just like the blood in her veins.

Through her sorrow, she blamed herself for dealing with a low-down, cheating bastard like Rick. The writing had been on the wall, but instead of walking away from him, she turned a blind eye and deaf ear to Rick's infidelities. Now Jaycee had to live the rest of her life knowing she would never be able to hold and kiss the baby that once grew inside her womb and whom she loved unconditionally, sight unseen.

The attending physician entered the room to review the results of all the tests and procedures performed on

Jaycee. As if she hadn't been through enough, she got another shock that made the blood in her veins turn to hot lava. Rick had given her gonorrhea that had gone untreated since she had no idea she was even infected. Because of that, there was little hope she would have carried the baby to full term. Even if the baby survived, the chances of it being born without serious medical conditions were slim to none.

Jaycee was confused because she was always a healthy woman. She had been good with going to her follow-up appointments at the doctor and never had any indication something was wrong. Her confusion then turned to anger at the thought of him sleeping with women unprotected and not being at all concerned about her health or that of her unborn child. Only time would tell how much damage had been caused or if she would ever be able to have children.

Just then, the nurse knocked on the door and said, "Ms. Maxwell, there's a young man outside who would like to see you. He says he's your boyfriend."

Jaycee's voice went up about ten octaves. "Fuck that lying-ass mutherfucka! I don't want to see that dirty dick bastard! Get him outta here!"

As the nurse opened the door to leave, Jaycee caught a glimpse of Rick standing outside of the room with a bouquet of roses. Jaycee tried to get up out of the bed, but she was hooked up to so many machines that she could barely move. The doctor moved toward Jaycee to restrain her.

"Ms. Maxwell, please calm down and get back in bed," said the doctor.

Then he turned to the nurse and gave her the directive to have security remove Rick from the hospital floor for as long as Jaycee was a patient in order to minimize her stress.

The door closed slowly. Through his tear-stained eyes, Rick saw the pure hatred Jaycee had for him as she made one last attempt to lunge her body toward the door. Suddenly, the pain from the intravenous needle stuck in her arm caused her to fall back into bed. Her mother sat next to her, trying to comfort her during what seemed to be a hopeless situation. Jaycee's heart raced as she took short, fast breaths to calm down. Never in her life had she ever felt as embarrassed and betrayed as she did at that moment.

Finally, reality set in. As she played back the events of the last few hours, it was obvious to Jaycee that her relationship with Rick was not healthy because he only cared about himself. He sure as hell wasn't thinking anything about her if he was willing to subject her to catching any and everything those scandalous tricks had as a result of his countless unprotected sexual encounters. Who knew what kind of father he would have been to their child. She had gotten so wrapped up in the fascination of his fast, lavish lifestyle that she didn't care he did the things he did behind her back...and sometimes in her face! She felt even dumber because she didn't follow her instincts to leave him alone a long time ago. Then, to lose the one thing she loved more than her own life was like someone had taken a knife and plunged it into her chest repeatedly, slowly killing her a million times. She knew for a while Rick was pure poison, but she just didn't want to face it.

Take No Prisoners

Jaycee jumped up from her bed as the alarm clock screamed, saving her from her fifteen-year-old nightmare. Tears formed in the corners of her eyes as she attempted to slow down her breathing. Her brows were covered with sweat.

Sucking her teeth, Jaycee rolled over slowly in her king-sized bed. While lying under her plush comforter and 500-count cotton sheets, she stared at the numbers as they blinked obnoxiously with a bright red glow. She hit the snooze button and looked up at the ceiling. Jaycee often thought about how different her life would be had she continued to play ignorant to the games, lies, and deception of Rick. That was the most painful lesson she had ever endured, and from that day on, her heart was hardened.

Sadly, Jaycee had to get up and endure another day filled with back-to-back meetings with pompous assholes who still thought the boardroom was no place for a woman, especially a black one. Nevertheless, Jaycee Maxwell was the baddest chick in the finance game. She was brains and swag all rolled into one. At thirty-eight, she was the youngest, senior-level stockbroker for RSM Investment Group, who single handedly brought in ten new multi-million dollar clients during her first year. It wouldn't be long before she reached the level of partner. There were at least five different men who had been with the firm for over twenty years who were in line for the title. After only being with the firm ten years, Jaycee let those old fossils know she was a force to be reckoned with. She always had on her game face, pimping corporate executives with her expert financial knowledge and her dashing wit. It didn't hurt that she was easy on the eyes, which men and women alike found appealing.

Jaycee was five-foot-six with a Coke bottle shape and a big ol' bubble that followed her around when she walked. She always flashed a winning smile that showed off her beautiful white teeth and deep dimples, which looked like holes on both sides of her face. Jaycee's grandmother nicknamed her "Hole in the Face" when she was just a little girl. Every time Jaycee went to visit her grandmother, she would take the knuckle of her index finger and twist it around inside her dimples before giving her a hug. Jaycee was closer to her grandmother than her own mother, and in Jaycee's mind, that nickname represented the special bond they shared that could never be broken. Her grandmother had been the only one allowed to call her that. To hear someone else call Jaycee "Hole in the Face" would have taken her back to a dark place on that cold October night when she heard her grandmother utter those words one last time before closing her eyes to the world. Just like her grandmother, that nickname was laid to rest.

It was no secret around the firm that Jaycee was the one who all the men desired. They loved to get a look at her ass as she walked up and down the halls of the office. When she knew they were looking, which was almost always, she would throw in a little extra swagger that made her ass jiggle. That was something her professors at Wharton School of Business didn't teach. If given the opportunity, her male co-workers would give up their prized possessions for a chance to get a peek, or better yet, a taste of what lie between her legs. Jaycee knew that, too, and used it to her advantage. She would set her eyes on a target and plan her strategy. Just when her prey was most vulnerable, she would pounce, catching them with their pants down as she finessed them out of investment opportunities. She would leave those poor souls completely stripped of their dignity while she laughed all the way to the bank. One thing was obvious.

She certainly was a killer shark in a sea of fish, devouring her competition one deal at a time.

When Jaycee started with RSM Investment Group ten years ago, she had an agenda––to seek and destroy, taking no prisoners...When she got promoted after her first year with the firm, she became the most hated, most feared woman at the firm, and that was how she liked it.

Jaycee finally dragged herself out of bed and turned on the Bose system that sat by her bedside. First, she listened to the weather and traffic reports. The two things she hated the most was not having her sexiness properly clothed for the weather and being late for work. Then, she turned on her favorite radio show, *The Steve Harvey Morning Show*. She continued to get dressed as she listened to the character "Tongue Tied" sing the hits. By far, this was one of her favorite segments of the show. Every word he sang always started with the letter "T", which made her holler out loud every time she heard him. Jaycee sang right along with Tongue Tied, mispronouncing all the lyrics just as badly.

While adding the finishing touches to her hair and makeup, "The Strawberry Letter" came on. It was about a woman who was crazy in love with a man who treated her like shit. This spoiled Jaycee's whole mood. She was sick to death of women with low self-esteem, falling in love with stupid-ass men that didn't have a pot to piss in or a window to throw it out of. Jaycee didn't have a man because she felt there was no one in the world of dating worthy enough of her time and attention. She thought, *Why should I bother? They can't give me anything I can't give myself!*

The few men she dated in the last year all had a weak sex game. She had yet to find someone who could make her toes curl and scream from excitement that would erupt from the pit of her stomach. Most importantly, she had never known true love, the type that made her feel like she was on cloud nine looking down at the poor suckers who wished they could be in her shoes for just a day. Jaycee opened herself up to what she thought was true love only once in her life. That illusion of love took her to a desolate valley just as devastating as losing her grandmother and almost cost her sanity.

For five long years, Jaycee loved Rick with her whole heart and soul. He definitely wasn't the ideal man her family would have chosen for her. He was a loud, thugged-out nigga who was quick to turn his head at the sight of another pretty face, tiny waist, big ass and perky double D's, and he didn't give a damn if anyone noticed. Jaycee was definitely a woman that any man would be honored to have on his arm, but Rick was a dog to say the least.

Rick and Jaycee came from two different worlds. She was a sheltered girl who came from a good upbringing. Her parents always encouraged her to shoot for the stars, and it showed through her many accomplishments both in and out of school. The streets were all Rick knew, which always seemed to puzzle Jaycee because he was so smart and witty——all the qualities possessed by a successful, legitimate businessman. Instead, he chose to swim in the belly of the drug underworld. After taking a gun charge at sixteen years of age and spending two years at the Youth Study Center, he quickly earned street credibility as the little nigga who took one for the squad.

Jaycee's father couldn't stand Rick any further than he could throw him, and he did everything in his power to keep him away from his daughter. He always told Jaycee, "Those little niggas are only out for one thing! Trust me, I was one once, and I know how they think!"

It didn't matter what Jaycee's father said, because it always went in one ear and out the other. She was determined to do what she wanted to do.

Rick was well known in the hood for being a pivotal force in the drug game. After serving his two-year sentence, he began moving up through the ranks and later became a boss moving millions of dollars in cash and narcotics. He was a very business savvy man who had the gift of gab. He could talk anyone into or out of anything.

Jaycee was also well known in the hood as Rick's girl. When niggas saw her coming, they knew not to fuck with her, otherwise Rick would set it off. His homies often jokingly questioned how Rick managed to pull someone as classy as Jaycee. They knew what kind of dude Rick was. He could talk anyone out of their drawls, if he so desired. Rick saw something in Jaycee that was different than the other hoes he dealt with. His goal was to make enough money so he could go legit, and when he did, he wanted to make sure he had someone like Jaycee on his arm. So, Rick treated Jaycee like a lady of a true baller and bought her anything she could ever want or need. She became comfortable with the jewelry, clothes, and cars that kept her flossing just like him. Whenever the time came for him to do his dirt, he would kindly excuse Jaycee so she wouldn't get caught up in his dealings.

When Jaycee turned twenty-three, she got pregnant. She was so excited! She forgot all about the fact that she was still in college and not in a position to care for a baby. When her parents found out, it was like World War III in the Maxwell home. Jaycee's father was furious and didn't speak to her throughout the entire first trimester. He even threatened to put her out, but luckily, her mother intervened. Jaycee's mother knew if her father put her out, she would only run straight to Rick. That meant she would have dropped out of school to take care of a baby who had a bastard for a father. Her parents had worked too long to see their daughter get so far in her college education, only to waste it on some thug and bring their grandchild up with the long arm of the law always banging at the door. So, Jaycee stayed home and continued to go to school.

Jaycee knew what type of dude she was dealing with, but in her mind, love conquered all. So, she often faked as if the rumors and suspicions of his dealings with other women didn't bother her. Whenever she confronted him with allegations of fucking around on her, he did what he did best——sweet talk her right out of her panties.

What Jaycee also found to be amazing was that during the time she spent wasting her life with Rick, she never experienced an orgasm. She instantly got mad because she had allowed herself to be sucked into all of that nonsense for a dick that didn't make her scream obscenities that could be heard throughout the neighborhood. That's when she discovered the next best thing——toys. She figured whenever she needed satisfaction, she could go to "The Mood" on South Street and invest in something long, hard, wide, and with a subtle vibration that took a lot of batteries but made her cum a river! So, in exchange for cumbersome relationships, she fell in love with money and power as she trumped bitch-ass wannabes who thought they were close to having bigger balls than her.

Jaycee stepped outside of her Wyncote home ready for battle on a beautiful April morning. Her black power suit was freshly pressed and tailored to fit every curve of her body. The red camisole underneath her blazer gave her just a pop of color that told others that she could be fun, but cross a bitch the wrong way and she would be the one to draw first blood. Her hair was a chestnut brown color with subtle blonde highlights, and she sported a nice bob-styled cut.

She jumped into her black Mercedes E-Class with burgundy leather interior that she affectionately called "Black Mamba" because it was the most lethal piece of machinery that ever hit the streets. She turned on the radio to catch the rest of the Steve Harvey show while heading down Washington Lane, preparing herself to hit some rush-hour traffic as she got closer to Lincoln Drive.

Reality Check

Jaycee arrived at the office with time to spare. She stepped off the elevator and walked toward her office with a confidence that signified she was a woman who could stomp with the big boys. Yet, she still walked, talked, and acted like a lady. As much as the men despised her, they couldn't help being mesmerized by the ghetto booty that swayed gracefully from side to side like the director of an orchestra as they played the perfect symphony. When she reached her office door, her assistant, Robyn, handed her a stack of messages and purchase requisitions that required Jaycee's signature. Out of everyone in the firm, Robyn was about the only person Jaycee associated with.

Robyn was almost fifteen years younger than Jaycee and working toward her Master's degree in business. Robyn was very bright, perceptive, and had the same hunger that reminded Jaycee so much of herself at Robyn's age.

Robyn's skin was a silky caramel complexion with an orange undertone that was beautifully accentuated whenever she wore warm colors. She was very shapely, with supple breasts that looked like they stood at attention about two feet away from her body. She didn't have as much wagon dragging behind her like Jaycee, but what Robyn lacked in that area, she definitely made up with her powerhouse legs that flexed whenever she walked. She looked as if she could crush a bowling ball between her legs with one squeeze. Her light eyes possessed a green hue that drove the men in the office crazy. Robyn rocked short hair cropped closely around the nape and sides. Long pieces came down from the crown of her head and swooped around her ears, blending in with the long asymmetric bangs that lay neatly across her forehead like her favorite singer, Rihanna. It gave her just the right amount of style and edge that was appropriate for the office and the club.

The one thing Jaycee admired the most about Robyn was her loyalty. Whenever one of those no-talent, whiny-ass, cry-baby colleagues either talked about Jaycee or made plans to do something underhanded, Robyn was always there to blow the whistle and catch those dumb asses with their pants down and cheeks hanging out in the breeze.

Almost daily, Jaycee and Robyn had light conversations about the nobodies Robyn dated and the disappointing mornings that resulted from the meaningless sexcapades she had the night before. Robyn always seemed to subject herself to random knuckleheads that were weak in bed, then come into work the next morning and complain to Jaycee about their shortcomings. From the dudes with little packages who couldn't make waves in a tub, to the two-minute brothers who left her even more sexually frustrated than before she let them have a crack at trying to get jack out of the box. Jaycee couldn't fathom why Robyn even bothered with those little boys.

Robyn had the potential to be a great entrepreneur, which was why Jaycee encouraged her to pursue her Master's degree. Her talents were indeed invaluable. She had a keen eye for detail. She was creative and a natural born leader. Jaycee thought Robyn's problem was she often confused her priorities by incorporating aspirations of a career while looking for that perfect love, which was always a no-no in Jaycee's book. Robyn was determined to go against the grain. She felt she could be successful and still find the man of her dreams. Unfortunately, in her quest to find Mr. Right, she came up short every time.

Nevertheless, Robyn's stories actually added a little comic relief to Jaycee's day. She got to listen to Robyn continuously play herself by dating men who were not worthy to share the same air with her. She was drawn to the neighborhood roughnecks, just like Jaycee had been in the past. Yet, Robyn still chased the fantasy that someday she would find love, as if it were standing at her front door all wrapped up with a red bow around it. In Jaycee's mind, finding that kind of love was wishful thinking.

As usual, Robyn came in with another bad date story. She followed Jaycee into her office and sat down. Before she spoke, Robyn gave Jaycee a long look. She waited for a signal of some kind to let her know Jaycee had time to talk before she started her day. Jaycee gave Robyn a little smirk, which was the green light for her to start dishing the dirt.

With a perplexed look on her face, Robyn said, "You know, I don't know why I put myself through this nonsense with these stupid-ass men! Just when I think I've found the one, something happens, and I can't pass go and collect two hundred dollars."

Jaycee looked at Robyn thinking, *What the hell is she talking about?*

Robyn continued describing her evening with her date.

"Everything seemed to be going well. We talked about everything from politics to sports. He was engaging, and

I thought, *finally*! So, the check comes, and he had the nerve to fix his lips to say, "Oh, baby...do you think you could cover this? I don't get paid until next week.'"

Jaycee wanted to laugh her ass off, but she continued to listen.

"So, I ended up paying the bill, which came up to about a hundred dollars..."

Jaycee stopped her. "You did what? What was in that food, crack? Come on now, you can't be that naïve! You're too intelligent for niggas like that to be running game on you. Get paid next week? Hell, I would've gotten up and kindly escorted my happy ass right on out the door, leaving *him* to figure out how he was gonna pay that bill!"

Jaycee couldn't believe what she had heard. It was women like Robyn––textbook smart but with no damn common sense––that pissed her off. Then the story got worse.

"When we got back to his house, we sat and watched old tapes of the *Little Rascals* in the rec room in his basement. He kissed me, and one thing led to another..."

Jaycee was on fire. She thought to herself, *No, this simple bitch didn't! This broke-ass nigga asks her out, she ends up paying the bill, and still gives up the coochie? Now, I'm convinced there was something in that food!*

Jaycee was so angry that the fine hairs on the back of her neck stood at attention as thoughts continued to race through her mind.

Does she want to have a man that bad that she's willing to dumb herself down just so she can appear to have something in common with that fool? And what the hell...tapes of the Little Rascals? How old is this man that he hasn't stepped up to updated movies and DVD's? This shit makes absolutely no sense at all!

Then, the coup de grace of the story sent Jaycee over the edge.

"Then, he hiked up my skirt, and we got it in on the couch. After about three minutes, he came and then started to cry as he hugged me real tight. He talked about how he'd never found anyone like me before. He told me how he wanted me to meet his mother and his children because he could see a future with me."

Jaycee snapped.

"Stop! I can't listen to any more of this shit. You gave up the booty on your dime? What the fuck is the matter with you? Does his mother and kids live with him, or is it the other way around? You'd better wise up if you expect to get everything you want in this business. I can tell you this much, you certainly won't get it by doing stupid shit like that!"

Robyn began to show signs of agitation.

"You can't expect every man to be sitting in his house with nothing to do except count stacks! I heard a woman on the Steve Harvey Morning Show one day say that she was told you shouldn't find a man with everything or he won't need you for anything," Robyn said sharply.

Jaycee smirked and said with confidence, "Which is exactly why I don't need men for anything! I can't believe you. This is by far the dumbest shit I have ever heard! The man you meet has got to be able to bring something to the table! You can't be the one doing everything. So, you keep that philosophy if you want to. In the meantime, you'll be dating some Joe Dickhead who's just milking your nest egg dry because he's always getting paid next week."

Becoming more annoyed with the condescending tone Jaycee took with her, Robyn decided to declare a war of words.

"I guess that's why you have cobwebs dangling from your pussy, 'cause you ain't gettin' any. So is this what being bitter and alone looks like?"

Jaycee was furious. Robyn had crossed the line from playful banter to blatant disrespect. Jaycee really wanted to step out of her heels and slap the shit out of her. However, unlike her subordinate, Jaycee had too much class. So, instead, she came back at Robyn in her business tone she often used with her colleagues when she was about to professionally rip them a new asshole, but what Jaycee said was in no way professional.

"Well, that's the difference between you and me. I don't spread my legs for every nigga that smiles and says hi. When you do find love, what do you think your man is going to say about the mileage you put on your tired, stretched-out pussy?"

Robyn rolled her eyes, went back to her desk, and proceeded to check the voicemail messages on the main office line. Her skin was as red as Jaycee's cami.

Jaycee gave a devilish grin and closed her office door. Then she sat down at her desk and started to go through her schedule for the day, while returning the messages that were left for her prior to her arrival at the office.

Although Robyn didn't say anything, their discussion was far from over.

I, De-Clare War

Jaycee may have won the battle of words with Robyn, but the war was far from over. She was still pissed off. Then, Jaycee realized she wasn't angry at the remark Robyn made about her being bitter and alone. It was the fact Robyn was just as young and naïve as she had been back in the day. By allowing herself to be sucked in to sleeping with every man she went out with, Robyn was on a slow, downward spiral that would leave her with no man, no baby, and no life...just like her! A few minutes later, Jaycee came to the conclusion that she had nothing to do with how Robyn lived her life. She felt if Robyn wanted to go fishing for little guppies in the hood that didn't have shit, didn't want shit, and therefore, couldn't give her shit, it was her prerogative. She was over it.

Jaycee continued on with her day. She was beginning to fade after her dreaded back-to-back morning meetings, but she kept her game face. For some reason, the words Robyn said to her earlier played over and over in her mind. Jaycee didn't always have negative feelings about relationships. In fact, she often welcomed the thought of having a boo who she could cuddle up with at night and watch a good movie or just have some mind-blowing sex. When Jaycee was a little girl, she used to imagine what her wedding would be like, from her gown to the place settings on the reception tables. She also pretended to cook dinner for her imaginary husband and children. She remembered getting her mom's apron that hung on a hook on the kitchen wall, putting it on, and going to town as she cooked her imaginary husband's favorite meal of fried chicken, macaroni and cheese, and collard greens. She smiled as she reminisced about a time of innocence...when life seemed easy and carefree.

As Jaycee got older, she was introduced to heartache, starring men as the arch nemesis and her as the damsel in distress. She wondered why her experiences with boys and men were so exhausting. In high school, she liked a boy named Omar, who ran on the track team. He was tall and slender, with smooth skin almost the color of amber. He had the most hypnotic eyes she had ever seen, light brown with huge black pupils. She found out the feeling was mutual, which excited her beyond measure.

Jaycee wasn't always a beautiful swan. Like any girl, she went through the ugly duckling phase, having a flat chest, skinny legs, and pimples. The boys would always look past her to goggle at the light-skinned girls with the tits and ass of grown women.

Jaycee and Omar dated from the end of their junior year up until the end of the summer. She did all kinds of things to show how much she liked him, such as buying cards and singing telegrams for his birthday with the money she earned from her part-time job at the mall. They even made plans to go to the senior prom together the following year. With all she had done, Jaycee was convinced she had this dude on lockdown. However, when she gave up the booty, that's when shit changed!

Two weeks before the start of their senior year, she went on a cruise to the Caribbean with her family. When she got back, that's when Omar dropped the bomb. Without rhyme or reason, he broke up with her. He just stopped talking to her. Like a bitch, he refused Jaycee's calls by having his mother lie for him, saying he wasn't home. Jaycee was devastated. Between the tears, she tried to understand what she did that made him not want her. That answer still remained a mystery long after she got over him.

Omar plus Rick equaled heartache. For Jaycee, the philosophy she heard over and over about the third time being a charm was bullshit! She had already felt pain twice in her life. That was more than enough ammunition for her to dodge a third bullet.

Weeks had gone by since Robyn shared any of her unpleasant experiences with broke-ass losers who lived with their mothers. Although Jaycee and Robyn were still civil toward one another, it was evident that after their last exchange, their alliance had been damaged. From that point on, it was strictly business between them, which suited Jaycee just fine. As a professional, she felt their relationship violated all boundaries of the workplace, which was a mistake Jaycee planned to never make again. Besides, Jaycee was about making money, and she didn't have time for socializing in the office anyway.

Jaycee didn't have many friends simply for the sake of living a so-called drama-free life. So, she referred to everyone as associates, and she tolerated them whenever she had the urge, which wasn't often. In fact, if she engaged in any type of conversation, it was about work and making money. Everything else was moot. She even alienated herself from her family because she thought they were always after her money, and she wasn't having that. She refused to allow her mooching-ass family borrow the money she worked so damn hard for, knowing she would never see it again. Jaycee only had contact with her parents, whom she loved dearly. She would go through the fire for them and only them.

Letting the Guard Down

Jaycee sat in her office on the phone while completing a few transactions for a client, when suddenly, a muscular shadow draped in a tailor-made blue suit glided past her door. On most days, Jaycee acted like the president and proud member of the She Woman, Man Haters Club, but on this day, she almost broke her neck trying to get a glimpse of the distinguished gentleman without being noticed. The unidentified man stood outside of Jaycee's office talking to Seth Rothman, one of the managing partners of the firm. The scent of Issey Miyake wafted into her office and straight up her nose, causing her pubic hairs to stand at attention.

As Seth continued to explain the company's history and impeccable reputation, the man had a slight grimace on his face as if Seth was boring him to tears. Jaycee tried to fake the funk like she wasn't interested in the man and all his sexual splendor. Yet, for the first time, her body was awakened, which intrigued her.

Seth wasn't really much of a whisperer, no matter how hard he tried. He just had that type of voice that projected all over the office. Jaycee didn't mind because it was more of an alert for her to duck and take cover so he wouldn't come into her office talking her to death. Whenever Seth came around, all he wanted to do was talk a hole in her brain about nothing she found to be interesting. Seth was very fond of Jaycee, and in so many ways, it was like Jaycee was his therapist.

Seth had a wife and three kids, and was always telling Jaycee stories about how over the top they were. His sixteen-year-old daughters were identical twins who fought all the time. It seemed like they hated each other. No one could believe that two people who looked exactly alike could have so much contempt for each other. Once, they fought so badly, they put holes in their bedroom door and ripped the phone off the wall just because one wanted to use it, but her sister was taking too long to hang up.

Seth's twelve-year-old son was a PlayStation junkie, who sat in his room like a zombie playing games and jacking off to the skin flicks on the Playboy channel. He only came out of the room when he had to shit, shower, eat, and go to school. Jaycee didn't understand why he even had cable in his room.

Seth always came to work complaining about how disrespectful his children were. They were always telling him to go fuck himself whenever he asked them to do anything. One would have to wonder if they were really his children. Jaycee thought, *How can anyone like Seth expect to gain any respect from his children when he's never home to lay the smack down whenever they get out of line?*

When Seth found himself stuck at home, all he did was make a fool of himself, trying desperately to bond with his children by dressing like a skater and using the latest slang. His wife sat around and watched television all day. In her mind, that was her job. Honestly, with the paper Seth brought home, working was the least of her concerns. If he asked her to do so much as straighten the magazines in the rack, she would look at him and jokingly say, "Surely you can't be serious! What the hell do we have a maid for?"

Jaycee always thought Seth's problem was he was too busy asking his family to do things, when he should have been telling them. To Jaycee, Seth was just a pussy who let his family run all over him. He was good at kissing their asses, showering them with money and expensive gifts, and staying up to his eyeballs with work. That was only way to keep the peace in his house.

Jaycee tuned into Seth's voice just in time to hear him say, "Oh, and here is one of our top employees,

Jaycee Maxwell! I'll tell ya' she's a natural when it comes to this business. She's been with us for only a short time, but if she keeps it up, it won't be long before she shoots right on up the corporate ladder."

Jaycee smiled with a sinister grin. It was about time someone gave her props for all of the cake she brought into the firm. Jaycee worked her ass off to get where she was, and she felt she deserved to be a partner.

Just as she looked up, the mystery man turned around, and their eyes met. The man gave her a sexy smile that caused her fluids to gush. Even Robyn looked at him and bit her fingernail seductively.

Under her breath, Jaycee uttered, "Damn."

Jaycee quickly turned away as she tried to regain her composure. Seth and the man walked into her office to conduct a formal introduction.

"Jaycee Maxwell, I'd like to introduce you to Ross Daniels. He is one of the top marketing executives in the city, and he's looking for a talented member of our team to handle his investments."

Jaycee looked him over and thought about how much she wanted to experience every inch of him with all five of her senses. For the first time, a man had her thinking about something other than work. In fact, Ross stirred feelings in her that she thought had been buried years ago. This made her uncomfortable.

What the hell is happening? This man walks in looking like butter, smiles, and I start to lose my cool? Am I slippin'? Naw, fuck that! I'm Jaycee Maxwell, bitch! she thought.

She quickly pulled herself together, looked at him, and flashed a fake smile.

"Hello. It's a pleasure to meet you, Mr. Daniels," Jaycee replied in a professional tone.

As Ross reached out to shake her hand, he said, "Please, call me Ross."

There was instant electricity as their skin met. His low, silky voice made her body shiver. What she really wanted to do was push Seth's punk ass out of the office and sit on Ross' face. After searching deep past her thoughts of how bad she wanted him to do her from the back, the bitch in her finally re-emerged.

"If it's all the same to you, I'd rather not," Jaycee responded. Then she rolled her eyes, returned to her desk, and picked up the phone to make a call.

Ross watched every movement of her body as she glided back to her desk. Her ass gently swayed from side to side against the lining of her skirt, which caused a soft swishing noise that had Ross in a trance. His eyes quickly moved upward as she sat down, hoping she didn't notice him checking her out.

Ross smiled seductively. "Well, it was a pleasure meeting you, Mrs. Maxwell..."

Jaycee interrupted coldly. "It's Ms. Maxwell. Mrs. Maxwell is my mother."

"Well then, Ms. Maxwell, how about you and I get together for dinner so we can talk about you handling my investments. That will give me time to see if you're as good as Seth here says you are," Ross replied calmly.

Jaycee had a bit of an attitude. She thought, *Oh, I know where this is going. You think I'm one of those weak bitches who doesn't have a clue, huh? You've got the wrong one!*

Jaycee thumbed through her desk calendar and said, "How about you and I get together in my office next week so we can discuss just how good I really am? My assistant will set you up."

Jaycee then proceeded to make her phone call.

Ross turned to look at Seth and said, "Well, well, well. She is definitely no nonsense about her business. I like that. I need someone like her to handle my business. At least I know I will be in good hands."

Seth's eyes lit up like it was Christmas. With the energy of a geeky kid, he said, "Yep! I told you she was good! That's why we love her!"

Jaycee looked over at Seth and thought, *Could he kiss my ass any harder?*

From her peripheral view, Jaycee caught Ross watching her every move as she talked on the phone. Ross' eyes studied Jaycee carefully as she took control of her phone call. Something inside her smiled. As much as she tried to ignore Ross, she couldn't deny the fact that he was sexy. Anyone would have been a fool not to think so. She remained cool, though. Then, out of nowhere, she decided to give him a show.

She spun around in her office chair and faced the window to take in the beautiful view of the blue sky and billowy clouds from the twenty-second floor. The sun hid behind one of the tall buildings, but still shined brightly over the people who walked on the street below. As she sat, Jaycee crossed her legs and began to play with her three-inch, Manolo Blahnik shoe as it dangled from her foot. While continuing with her conversation, she caught Ross still standing in her doorway, watching her as if she were a piece of candy that he would do anything to suck on.

Jaycee selfishly turned her chair around, completely facing the window. Ross detected that she was playing a little cat and mouse game, so he decided to engage her. Ross kindly excused himself, while Seth stood there going on and on about the integrity of the company and how much of an asset Jaycee would be to him if she handled his investment portfolio. Ross' view of Jaycee had him hypnotized. After a while, Seth's voice seemed like meaningless babble, like the teacher from the old Charlie Brown cartoons. He was determined to persuade Jaycee to go out with him.

Ross walked closer to Jaycee's door and gently knocked to get her attention. When Jaycee turned around, she saw the most beautifully put together man she had ever seen. Suddenly, it felt like her head was in conflict with her body. Her head told her that she didn't have time for him. She was not the type of female that tripped over men, no matter how good they looked. On the flip side, her body told her that she was long overdue for a marathon fuck session! Jaycee wanted to smile, but there was a force that instantly changed her smile to a stone-cold stare.

"Excuse me, Ms. Maxwell. I'm sorry to interrupt. Listen, I know you're busy, but I just had to tell you that you are absolutely stunning, and I really would like to get to know you better. How about you and I meet for a drink at the restaurant downstairs after you get off work?"

"And *why* do you feel it's necessary to get to know me better, Mr. Daniels?" Jaycee replied coldly.

"Well, Ms. Maxwell, I feel that since you're going to be handling my portfolio––"

"Wait a minute! Who told you that I was handling your portfolio?" Jaycee interrupted.

"I just assumed that since you came highly recommended, you would have no problem handling my business transactions," Ross said.

"Well, Mr. Daniels, you know what they say about people who assume. Besides, I really don't have time," Jaycee replied sarcastically.

For about thirty seconds, Ross and Jaycee were locked in a stare down. The more Jaycee looked at him, the more she felt the man in the boat between her legs pulsating, but she didn't break. If there was one thing she made very clear to her male clients, it's that she was not to be taken lightly.

Growing tired of the awkward silence, she sighed and said, "I have lots of work to finish. So, if you don't mind, you can see yourself out."

Ross smiled as he conceded to her request. "Okay, okay. I can see there's no changing your mind. So, no dinner and no drinks, but I would like for you to handle my investments. For that, I'm not taking no for an answer."

Jaycee couldn't believe Ross' persistence.

Okay, I've been rude to this man, turned down his dinner and after-work drink invitations, and he still wants me to work for him? Is he a glutton for punishment? she thought.

Her feelings of irritation slowly turned into flattery. Then, Jaycee finally said, "Alright, Mr. Daniels. If I handle your accounts--and that's a big 'if'--I will have Robyn contact you to set up an appointment in my office next week to go over a few things."

Ross gave a sly, half smile and said confidently, "Fair enough. It was a pleasure to meet you, Ms. Maxwell, and I'll be awaiting the call."

"You do that, Mr. Daniels," Jaycee replied.

Ross turned slowly and strolled away from Jaycee's office, heading for the elevator. Jaycee sat at her desk staring into space, unsure of what had just taken place. This man kept coming at her no matter how many times she turned him down. It was true that Jaycee had an impeccable reputation at the firm, but what shook her up was his passive-aggressive demeanor. She found this to be an attractive quality, which made her even more inclined to find out more about him.

* * * * *

As Jaycee eluded in their first encounter, she contacted Ross to discuss how her financial expertise could be employed to build upon his existing wealth. From the first day they met, Ross was already sold that she was vicious when it came to handling business. Jaycee traded aggressively, and she was good at it. She knew when to strike when the iron was hot, and she knew when to cut her losses and walk away from an investment unharmed. Being in a fast-paced environment where she could make a shitload of money in a matter of minutes made her nipples hard.

In the first few weeks of Ross being Jaycee's client, she almost tripled his money. This was especially good for her. The more she made for him, the more she made for herself. Jaycee was on a roll. She was more focused than she'd ever been in her life. She was sure her performance over the quarter would certainly land her the partnership in the firm.

Everything that Glitters Ain't Gold

It was a beautiful morning. The birds were chirping and the flowers were in full bloom, indicating that summer was in the air. As Jaycee took a scenic route to work through Fairmount Park, she saw a family of geese walking through the grass headed for the pond that sat right off Belmont Avenue. For the first time in a long while, she did not dread going into the office. Her appointment to meet with her favorite client, Ross Daniels, had a lot to do with it. Since she began working with Ross, there had been a drastic change in her mood. At times, she was still a bitch, but overall, her behavior seemed to be more pleasant, which was a side of her that no one in the office had ever seen before.

Word spread that it was Ross who had her stank attitude in check. Judging by the conversations held by the water cooler, everyone was ecstatic. Ross was doing something that created a change in her. The employees didn't give a damn what he did. They were just glad they didn't have to deal with her uppity attitude.

Jaycee entered the office looking especially fine, dressed in her lightweight, cream linen suit with a chocolate-colored camisole that hugged her torso ever so gently. Her shoes had the appearance of a linen texture with hints of chocolate that complemented her ensemble. She walked in with a pleasant look on her face and sent a barrage of "Good Mornings" that echoed through the halls. People weren't sure what this meant, but they took it all in stride. Jaycee walked into her office and placed her purse on the desk. Before she could sit down, Robyn entered the office.

"Excuse me, Jaycee. Seth would like to meet with you today."

Jaycee's body stiffened. She wondered if this was the news she had been waiting to hear for the last few months.

"No problem," she replied. "How am I on time today?"

"Surprisingly, your schedule is pretty light," Robyn told her. "You have an eleven o'clock appointment with Jessica Rothschild, a one o'clock with Jamison Johnson, and a three o'clock with Ross Daniels."

Jaycee checked her BlackBerry to make absolutely sure that she had no conflicts. Then, she looked at Robyn and said, "Okay, tell Seth that I can meet with him this morning at ten, and if that's no good, I'll push my lunch back and squeeze him in at noon. That will be all, Robyn. Thank you."

Although she dismissed Robyn abruptly, for the first time, Jaycee cracked a smile, which was not a usual occurrence since their falling out. Nevertheless, Robyn took it for what it was worth and went on about her business.

Two minutes later, the phone rang. Jaycee's phone always rang differently when an outside call came in. She didn't give out her direct number very often. When she did, it was because she was able to endure talking to that person for more than thirty seconds.

Jaycee picked up her phone, and in the most pleasant voice, she said, "Good morning! This is Jaycee. How may I help you?"

A sexy, baritone voice responded, "Well, good morning to you, Sunshine! You sound like you're having a good morning. I hope I had something to do with this jovial mood. Now, if you would only let me take you to dinner, you would make a brotha very happy."

Jaycee felt herself smiling. She almost broke down and accepted his invitation, but she had to remember Ross was still her client. Therefore, she had to keep it professional. She didn't need her nosey-ass colleagues talking behind her back, assuming there was more than a business relationship between she and Ross. She already suspected there was a buzz around the office about the two of them secretly being involved with each other.

"And, Mr. Daniels...to what do I owe this pleasure? Our meeting isn't until later on this afternoon. Is there something specific you need that requires my professional expertise prior to our meeting?" Jaycee said in a sexy, playful voice.

"Well, as a matter of fact, I do. When are you gonna let me eat strawberries and whipped cream off your entire body?" Ross replied.

Ross' statement caught Jaycee completely off guard. Her mind instantly pictured the scenario, which made her wet with excitement. She felt her guard coming down slowly, and that was rare. For a brief moment, she allowed herself to feel a hint of sexual stimulation, but she was not going to let his fine ass knock her off her square. She didn't want to let her desires cloud her judgment.

With a soft tremble in her voice, Jaycee said, "Mr. Daniels, let me reiterate that our relationship is strictly in the interest of your financial investments. So, I would appreciate it if you would refrain from making inappropriate statements such as the one you just made."

Ross knew he struck a nerve. "Then why did you take so long to respond? You sounded like you just finished releasing some built-up aggression and needed a cigarette."

Jaycee was caught. It was almost as if Ross were a fly on her wall, watching every move she made. She hated to admit that he was beginning to get under her skin.

Just then, Robyn came up to the door and knocked.

"Excuse me again, Jaycee."

Jaycee was slightly annoyed, but Robyn's timing couldn't have been any better.

"I'm sorry, but I have to go now," she told Ross. "I will speak with you soon."

Ross chuckled and replied, "Yes, ma'am. I will see you at three o'clock sharp."

Jaycee quickly hung up the phone and focused all of her attention on Robyn, who was still standing at the door waiting to deliver her message.

"Yes, Robyn?"

"I just wanted to let you know that Seth confirmed your meeting for ten o'clock this morning."

"Okay, thanks."

Jaycee sat at her desk in a mild trance after her brief, yet intense conversation with Ross. She didn't understand why he was getting to her. She did everything she could to keep their relationship strictly professional. However, she was having a hard time keeping her unspoken feelings suppressed. Her female intuition sensed Ross knew that, too, which is the reason why he kept insisting on seeing her outside of the office.

Suddenly, Jaycee pulled herself together and prepared for her meeting with Seth, which would be in ten minutes.

* * * * *

Excitement began to build as Jaycee walked the long corridor from her office down to the big conference room where she was scheduled to meet with Seth. She hoped this was the meeting that would change her career for the better.

She slowly opened the conference room door. Seth was already waiting for her. He had a look on his face that she had never seen before. Seth always seemed to be a happy kind of guy, especially when he was away from his family who stressed him out beyond measure. On this day, Seth sat in the chair looking almost emotionless.

Immediately, Jaycee's facial expression mirrored Seth's. She sat down slowly, never taking her eyes off his face. There was a moment of silence before Seth began to speak, which made Jaycee a little nervous. Something deep down within her psyche told her that this meeting was not going to be a good one. So, Jaycee prepared herself and went into her attack position she always presented in the conference room, leaning forward with her body forming a perfect ninety-degree angle in her chair. Her hands were folded as she prepared to pounce on him.

"Jaycee, I know we don't always see eye to eye on some things, but overall, I think you have done a hell of a job during your time with the firm. You are part of the reason why RSM Investment Group is where it is today, and for that, I thank you."

Jaycee replied, "Well, thank you, Seth. That means a lot coming from you." She really wanted to smile, but she felt there was a "but" coming, so she maintained her position.

Seth continued. "After an extensive review of all the candidates for partner in the firm, the board of directors has offered it to Bob Sanderson."

Bob Sanderson was a skinny little white guy who had been with the firm for twenty-five years. He reminded Jaycee of an ass-kissing little wimp, much like Seth. A blanket of red fell on the entire room through Jaycee's eyes. She tried to keep her professional composure, but it was hard to restrain the hood in her. Jaycee tried to sound calm, but her teeth were clenched together and her voice was flat.

"After all the revenue I have brought to this firm, how in the hell could you choose Bob Sanderson over me? I've done more for this company in the ten years I've been here than Bob has done during his entire tenure! I'm still wondering why he's still here!"

"Now, Jaycee, hear me out. Believe me, I fought for you tooth and nail with the board on this, but what it boiled down to was the fact that Bob has been here longer and his performance has been consistent over his time here," Seth explained.

Jaycee's voice began to elevate. "Well, I don't think you fought hard enough, and you should go back to the board and talk to them about reconsidering their decision! This is bullshit! Look at my track record! I'm clearly the better choice for partner! What is the board afraid of...a little color, estrogen...or both! I've worked too damn hard for my career to come down to this!"

"Jaycee, this has nothing to do with your race or gender. Yes, your performance over the last ten years has exceeded expectations. You're not afraid to take risks, but the board feels that some of your business tactics may be a little too risky, which could have a negative impact on the firm as a whole," Seth replied.

"Isn't that what the stock market is all about, taking risks?" she yelled. "Come on, Seth! You should know being safe and careful never makes money! It's all a gamble!

Seth calmly replied, "Well, unfortunately, the board is not ready for your philosophy. I'm sorry, Jaycee. The decision is final. Maybe in a few years——"

Jaycee quickly cut him off, refusing to hear Seth's next statement of waiting for another opportunity. "Too risky, huh? You didn't think I was being too risky all those late nights when I was in your office sucking on your old, shriveled-up dick that can't stay hard for more than two minutes! I wonder what your wife would think if she found out the real reason why you worked late all the time."

Seth began to grow angry. His brow crinkled downward. "Are you threatening me? Listen, Jaycee, I watch everything around here. You are very good at what you do, but not that good. You really don't want to go down that road with me."

Jaycee pushed her chair away from the table, got up, and stormed out of the conference room. When she got to her office, she gathered her things to leave. Robyn looked up, not sure of what just happened.

She quickly asked, "Jaycee, what's going on?

"I'm leaving! What does it look like?" Jaycee replied loudly.

Confused, Robyn asked, "When should I expect you back?"

"Cancel all my appointments! I'm not coming back today! Hell, I may not come back tomorrow either!"

Before Robyn could ask any more questions, Jaycee snatched up her belongings, slammed her office door, and disappeared into the elevator.

Jaycee's speedometer tipped over ninety-five miles per hour as she tore down I-76. Tears were streaming down her face so fast that they almost blinded her. She had just been handed the biggest slap in the face of her career. With all of the time and dedication she put into the firm, she was passed over for a man who she thought didn't have a clue of what it took to get ahead. No matter how many times Seth denied the allegations of racism and sexism, deep down, Jaycee knew their decision was based on the fact that she was the wrong color and didn't have a third leg.

Time for Some Action

Jaycee got home in record time. Surprisingly, the police didn't stop her. At the speed she drove, she could have had both the Philadelphia Police Department and the Pennsylvania State Troopers in hot pursuit, ready to hand her big fat speeding tickets. Regardless of how fast she drove, it still felt like it took an eternity for her to get home.

Finally, Jaycee pulled into her driveway, where she sat in her car for a moment trying to figure out her next move. After almost thirty minutes, she came to the conclusion that as long as RSM Investment Group was a male dominated, predominantly white firm, there was no chance in hell that she was going to get any further than where she was. It was okay for her to make the firm millions of dollars as long as she remained in the background. To have her as a partner, participating in major decisions that involved the overall direction of the firm, gave her way too much power than what those white men were willing to relinquish.

Jaycee needed a plan, but she was too consumed with her own emotions. So, she decided to take a few days just to clear her head. She wanted to make sure when she sat down to plan the next steps of her life, her decisions were not based strictly on emotion; but she was so angry she could spit fire! She needed an outlet after the rollercoaster ride she just endured. Since it was still early, she decided to put work aside and relax for the rest day. She wasn't going to focus on anything that had to do with work.

When Jaycee got inside the house, she walked over to her office, closed the door, and proceeded to plan a day of total serenity. As long as the office door was closed, she wouldn't be tempted to start working.

Jaycee contacted a spa service that provided in-home treatments. She was in the mood for a complete spa treatment, which included a meal. For full spa service in the home, it should have been reserved in advance, but since Jaycee knew the owner and was willing to pay whatever extra money was required to make her request happen, it was no problem. Like any other business, as long as the cash was green,, her request was happily honored.

After talking with Nelda, the owner of the spa service, Jaycee had everything she needed to have a relaxing day at home within two hours. Technicians and therapists set up stations in different rooms throughout Jaycee's house, giving it the look and feel of an actual spa. This was something Jaycee did for herself on occasion. It spared her from the idle chitchat she would have endured when in the presence of other spa guests.

Finally, everyone was in place, and Jaycee was ready to partake in a relaxing afternoon with the hope of removing the stress of the day. She changed into her big, fluffy, white robe that she only used for her in-home spa treatments. When she came downstairs, the smell of lavender filled the air. The aroma from the calming scent hypnotized her. Jaycee didn't realize until that very moment how much she was in dire need of a mental health day.

She moved slowly toward the massage table located in her den. Soothing melodies of spa sounds flowed through the speakers that were located in every room of the house. The massage therapist greeted Jaycee with a smile.

"Hello, Ms. Maxwell! My name is Holly, and I will be performing your massage today. Just lie down and relax, and I will take care of everything. Okay?"

Holly was about five foot nothing and looked like she weighed no more than a hundred pounds. She wore huge coverings on her hand that looked like fuzzy oven mitts to keep her hands warm.

Jaycee gave Holly a labored smile as she lay down on the table. Her body felt stiff and achy. Her shoulders felt like they weighed a ton. When Jaycee looked into the mirror situated over the couch, she could have sworn they were even with her ears. The small of her back screamed for relief as she tried hard to get comfortable on the table.

She wrestled with her thoughts about how she would get even with the bastards who did her dirty. It was painfully obvious to Jaycee that she was never going to get anywhere if she stayed at the firm. She concluded that whatever moves she made for her future would not include putting another damn dime into the pockets of Rothman, Stein, and Martin Investment Group.

Before another thought crept into Jaycee's mind, Holly removed the mitts and reached for the bottle of massage oil that sat in a warmer on the table. She poured the oil into the palm of one hand, rubbed both hands together, and then softly massaged the oil into Jaycee's skin. Holly found a pressure point with her thumb and index finger that put Jaycee into a relaxed trance, leaving her body vulnerable. She was amazed someone as tiny as Holly was strong as she was to subdue her. Without resistance, her body fully embraced the moment. The music sensually danced through her ear canals and soothed her mind.

Four hours later, Jaycee felt rejuvenated. She sat on her couch enjoying a wonderful snack of ground turkey wrapped in lettuce and a glass of water with lime and ginger that had been prepared for her by the spa service. She looked around at all of the beautiful things she worked her tirelessly to buy without the help of a man. Jaycee felt she was destined for greatness, but she also realized in order for that to happen, she had to be her own boss. She was tempted to go into her office to begin planning her strategy to bury those who were trying to hold her down.

Jaycee made a promise to herself to keep the office door closed for the day, and after wrestling with the idea for about five minutes, she gave in and decided to stay true to her promise. She had such a wonderful afternoon of pampering that she didn't want any thoughts of work to spoil her mood. She curled up with the stereo remote, shuffled through her CD changer, and found some Paul Hardcastle. As "Walking to Freedom" played, she stretched out on the couch and took a much-needed nap.

After a restful slumber, Jaycee was awakened by a loud, rumbling noise deep in the pit of her stomach. She glanced at the clock on the wall. It read 7:00 p.m. No wonder her stomach was screaming; it lacked sustenance. Jaycee was about to go to bed hungry because she was exhausted and didn't feel like cooking. She also didn't like going to bed on a full stomach. That was one surefire way to put on unwanted pounds, and

Jaycee was not trying to have her Coke bottle shape disappear under any circumstances. Her body was one of her most valuable assets, and just like her money, she treasured it. Unfortunately, she was hungrier than a hostage. Had she gone to bed, she would have dreamed of nothing but food. So, skipping a meal was not an option.

It was times like these when she wished she had a man to either take her out for a nice candlelight dinner down by the waterfront or cook for her at home. Afterwards, for dessert, he would cover her body in whipped cream and lick her from the top of her head to the soles of her feet. Then, she would feast on a midnight snack of chocolate-covered tube steak.

Knowing lying on the couch would not satisfy her hunger, Jaycee called in an order for dinner from a restaurant in Jenkintown. It was a reputable place owned by one of her clients, whom she made a very wealthy man. As a token of his appreciation, he prepared meals for Jaycee and had them specially delivered to her home.

While waiting for her dinner to arrive, Jaycee went into her basement to select a bottle of wine to go with her meal. It was fully furnished with a fifty-inch flat-screen television, surround sound system, exercise equipment, a butter-cream leather living room suite, and pool table. Jaycee had it hooked up to look like a mini apartment. It was another one of her personal places of peace aside from her office and bedroom.

At the front of the basement were double doors that led to a small storage space where she kept her wine collection. Jaycee kept at least seventy-five to a hundred bottles of wine. After she perused her selections, she decided on Italian Chianti to go with her T-bone steak, garlic roasted potatoes, and steamed vegetables.

Since it would be about forty-five minutes before her dinner arrived, she decided to pop the bottle open and have a glass as an appetizer. The first sip traveled down her throat nice and smooth, creating a warm sensation in the center of her chest. She continued to sip as Luther Vandross sang to her through the Bose system. Jaycee poured another glass of wine as sang back to the speakers.

"Don't you remember you told me you loved me, baby…"

After about six songs, Jaycee had consumed almost the whole bottle and was feeling no pain. She began to reflect on her life and whether or not she was truly happy. She had a promising career and money to maintain a lifestyle most women would have sold their souls to have. Still, there was emptiness within her, a void that couldn't be filled with material things.

It had been a while since Jaycee and Robyn had their falling out, but she still thought back to what Robyn said about her being bitter and alone.

I have everything I could possibly want and need, she thought. *So why do I feel like shit? Am I really going to end up bitter and alone?*

Jaycee's heart felt like it sank to the pit of her stomach. So, she polished off the last of the wine to relieve the uneasy feeling. She figured drowning her sorrows in the bottle was the only solution.

When the doorbell rang, Jaycee stumbled to the door and opened it. The deliveryman stood at the front door with her food in hand. She took the bag, tipped him, and quickly shut the door. While walking toward the couch, Jaycee went through the bag to make sure everything was there. She discovered the deliveryman forgot the homemade rolls that accompanied every meal. She really didn't need them that late in the evening, but it was a guilty pleasure she couldn't resist. Quickly, she stumbled back toward the door to catch him. She flung the door open, and much to her surprise, Ross was standing there looking just as sexy as the day she met him.

"Hello, Ms. Maxwell!" Ross said in his sexy, Barry White tone.

He was dressed in a cream linen pants set. Crisp and clean with a pair of brown gators, he looked and smelled just like money. He was clean-cut like a sophisticated man should be. Despite the fact Jaycee felt her juices gushing at the sight of him, she was plenty pissed that he was standing at her door. She never allowed her clients to know where she lived, and she surely didn't like when people stopped by unannounced, even if they looked like Ross.

Before he could say anything, Jaycee quickly slipped back into bitch mode. With a heavy tongue, Jaycee unleashed her drunken venom.

"What are you doing here, Mr. Daniels? Better yet, how did you find out where I lived, because I sure as hell didn't tell you? Did Robyn tell you how to find me? If so, I will personally see to it that she's fired!"

Ross gave her a sly smile and said, "No, Robyn did not tell me where you lived. Why do you sell me short? It's not like I don't know people. I have my own connections that can get me the information I need when I need it. How do you think I got where I am today?"

"Regardless, you have no business being here and you need to go," Jaycee said, while almost tripping over the doormat.

Ross stood at her door with a look of genuine concern for Jaycee. He knew she had an air about her that often turned people off, but there was something about her that intrigued him and made the soldier in his pants tingle.

When Ross did not adhere to her demand, she became belligerent. In her drunken state, Jaycee pushed Ross with every ounce of strength she had and yelled, "Nigga, didn't I tell you to get the fuck away from my door? Leave me alone!"

Ross' concern turned to anger. The only professional and sophisticated man to grace her doorstep in what seemed to be ages suddenly went straight hood. He gripped Jaycee up by her left arm.

"Get the fuck off me!" she yelled. "You gonna come to my motherfuckin' house and disrespect me by puttin' yo' hands on me?"

She drew her right arm back and swung, aiming right for his face. Ross did the move from the *Matrix*, leaning backwards to dodge her swing that seemed to be powerful judging from the gust of air he felt as her fist flew past his face. Suddenly, Ross grabbed Jaycee's right arm, leaving her defenseless if he were to retaliate.

"Yo, you better calm the fuck down!" Ross yelled.

Anger was written all over Ross' face. His brows crinkled, and his upper lip curled like he was getting ready to knock her ass out. Jaycee's eyes grew wide as the bass in his voice vibrated through her chest.

"I came by to see how you were doing because I heard about what happened today. See, that's the problem with you corporate women! You're always on the defensive because you think someone is always out to get you. Meanwhile, you treat a good brother like shit! I don't know why I even bothered to show any kind of concern for your stuck-up ass! Now I understand why everybody thinks you're such a bitch! Your head is so far up your own ass that you can't even tell when muthafuckas are trying to show you an ounce of kindness! You've been nothing but a snob since the day I met you!"

Still holding her tight, Ross' nostrils flared as he continued.

"Then, you raise your hands to me? You'd better be glad you didn't try that shit five years ago, or the outcome would have been very different! It's women like you who settle for those nut-ass niggas who dog them out, yet they stay and deal with the bullshit! Then after they've used them up, the woman becomes scorned. So when a good one comes along, they wanna make their life a living hell, acting like a nigga owes them something. They expect brothers like me to kiss their ass! Well, I'm telling you right now I'm not that dude. I'm not gonna chase you!"

As Ross turned to walk away, Jaycee slumped down in the doorway and started to cry. She knew everything Ross said about her was true. Indeed, she was that typical woman, scorned by past loves that caused her to close her heart in order to save herself from reliving that pain ever again.

When Ross walked into Jaycee's office for the first time, she felt something for him. No matter how hard she tried to conceal it, Ross was the perfect image of the man she often dreamed about but never thought she'd find.

As Ross turned the corner toward the driveway, Jaycee yelled helplessly, "Wait! Please don't leave!"

Ross stood next to his shiny, black Cadillac Escalade, contemplating whether or not he was going to take a chance on her and go back. In his mind, he thought, *Fuck this! I don't need this nonsense.*

However, some mystical, magnetic force working against Ross pulled him back in the direction of Jaycee's front door. So, instead of him getting in his truck and driving away, Ross slowly walked back to the house, hoping he wasn't being a sucka for buying into her tears. When he reached the clearing, Jaycee was still in her doorway, sobbing uncontrollably.

For about thirty seconds, Ross stood there watching her, unsure of what he wanted to do. He wondered if he attempted to help Jaycee back into the house, would she try to chin check him, or would she finally welcome his assistance without feeling he had an ulterior motive. While Jaycee sat motionless like a rag doll on her doorstep, Ross leaned down over her. His dark shadow hovered over her like a protective shield. This time, he gently took her arm and lifted her off the ground. Jaycee's legs felt weak. She tried to stand up, but she just didn't have it in her. For the first time in a very long time, Jaycee allowed herself to lean on someone else to help her to stand. Jaycee's robe was twisted, exposing a significant amount of cleavage that caught Ross' eye.

He slid his hand around her waist, guided her into the house, and shut the door. He then walked her into the den and sat her down on the couch. As Ross gently laid Jaycee onto the couch, she reached up, placed both hands around his muscular neck, and pulled him closer to her lips. Before Ross could realize what was happening, Jaycee forcefully planted her tongue in his mouth and massaged his with fire and passion. Jaycee wasn't sure if what she had done was right, but the scent of his cologne had her clit throbbing. At that moment, she wanted to smell, taste, and feel him inside of her.

A gambler by nature, Jaycee decided to take her chances of finding out if the saying about men with big feet was true. For a split second, she worried about how Ross would look at her afterwards. Then, she figured she could pretty much say or do anything and get away with it because she was blitzed out of her mind. If Ross ever tried to jog her memory, she could fake amnesia and blame her behavior on the alcohol.

Ross reciprocated the kiss and reached inside Jaycee's robe to massage her breasts that lay comfortably tucked away in a black lace Victoria's Secret bra. Her nipples were suddenly awakened by the gentle touch of his hands, which were so soft. It was like he had never done manual labor in his life.

It didn't take much for Ross to quickly become aroused. He eagerly anticipated the moment when he would be ready to inject himself into her body like an I.V. to a vein. He wanted to give Jaycee what she had missed and desired for so long.

As the sensuous sounds of Donell Jones sang to her, Jaycee went for Ross' shirt. She ran her hands across his perfectly sculpted chest that sent a chill throughout her body. Aggression overwhelmed her, and without thought, she pulled her arms outward while they were still under Ross' shirt and ripped the buttons clean off, exposing a beautiful work of art that was gift wrapped in a smooth, milk chocolate package. Ready to slip himself inside her, Ross' manhood grew bigger, longer, and harder. Between Jaycee's legs was a river that ran deep, and she wanted Ross to be the one who braved the raging waters. There was no turning back for either of them.

Ross undid Jaycee's robe and began kissing her. He started from her forehead and traveled downward. During his journey, he undid her bra and sucked on her nipples. He continued downward, running his tongue across her tight abs. Jaycee's stomach muscles contracted from the sensation of his tongue as he made his descent to her hidden treasure. She wanted him to sex her so badly that she tried to pull him back up so they could skip the formalities of foreplay. But, this was something Ross took pride in, and he was not going to let her take control of this moment. In his mind, he was the boss, not Jaycee. Ross pinned her hands down on the couch as he continued his way toward her pot of gold.

Jaycee was going insane, and after drinking a whole bottle of wine, everything she felt was amplified twenty times. She closed her eyes as she felt the tickle of his tongue slowly approach her bikini line. When Ross reached his destination, Jaycee forgot all about acting like a lady as he licked, sucked, and kissed the nectar that flowed freely from her body.

Once Ross was good and ready, he came up for air and gently pushed his stiff rod into her juicy cave. Jaycee's eyes widened and then closed as she took in all of him with pleasure.

She couldn't believe she was there with Ross, a man whom she often fantasized about no matter how much she tried to fight it. Most of all, she couldn't believe that after months of the river being dried up, she was finally getting broke off a little something.

Ross took Jaycee's legs and rested them on his shoulders. He watched as she made the faces of sexual pleasure that would give any man an ego boost. With every rhythmic stroke, Jaycee let out a melodious moan that made him plunge deeper and faster into her. Suddenly, Ross flipped Jaycee onto her hands and knees and proceeded to work her from behind. This was truly the mind-blowing, toe-curling sex that she had waited for all her life.

Getting a side glimpse of Ross from the mirror in the den, she watched as all the muscles in his body worked in unison to make her feel good. Then, Jaycee felt her walls beginning to contract. Ross felt it, too. His strokes quickened.

As they were both getting ready to release screams of passion that would be heard across town, Jaycee moaned, "Ooh, baby!"

While Ross continued to stroke her walls with care, the words Jaycee thought she would never utter again slipped from her lips as she reached ecstasy.

"I...I...I love you!"

Jaycee's body convulsed as her juices polished Ross' member. He couldn't hold back anymore. Besides, he had accomplished his task—making sure Jaycee exploded with pleasure. So, with one last thrust, Ross grabbed Jaycee's hair. His back arched, flexing all of his muscles as he released his load like a gladiator. He shivered and then he rolled over onto his back, pulling Jaycee on top of him. He ran his hands down the small of her back and kissed her lips softly.

Jaycee forgot all about her dinner. It didn't even matter, because Ross satisfied a greater hunger that food never could. They lay there motionless as fatigue took over and sent them into a seductive slumber.

It's About To Go Down

Riiiinnnnng! The alarm clock went off at 8:45 a.m.

"Shit!"

Robyn jumped up, her body dripping with sweat. Her heart raced as she tried to catch her breath. The dream about Jaycee seemed way too real, and Robyn wondered what it all meant. Unfortunately, Robyn didn't have time to sit around and process her thoughts because she was late as hell. She was due to be in the office by nine o'clock. This was the third time in a week she would be late, and she knew tardiness drove Jaycee insane.

"I know this bitch is gonna give me a hard time today," she said to herself, while running to the phone to call the office.

A cheerful woman answered.

'Good morning, RSM Investment Group...Carol speaking. How may I help you?"

Robyn had to think quickly. She didn't want Carol to report back to Jaycee that she had overslept, so she went with the classic reason why people ran late.

"Carol...Hey, it's Robyn! Listen, I'm running late. My car won't start, and I'm waiting for Triple A to come and give me a jump. Would you let Jaycee know I'll be in as soon as I can?"

"Sure, Robyn!" Carol happily replied. "I'll give her the message."

"Thanks, Carol. I should be in before ten," Robyn told her.

In her comforting, mom-like manner, Carol said, "Will do, honey! See you soon! Bye-bye now!"

Carol, the receptionist, was an older woman who had worked for the firm for what seemed to be forever. She always had a cheerful disposition and everyone loved her. Even when Jaycee was in the bitchiest of moods, she couldn't help but smile whenever Carol greeted her.

Robyn hung up the phone and jumped in the shower. Deep down, she knew today was not going to be the best of days.

It was quarter after nine, and surprisingly, Robyn was fully dressed and ready to go. She would have never gotten ready for work that fast on a good day. She always had good intentions by getting up early, but somewhere along the way, she would always end up making a mad dash out of the house, barely making it to work on time.

Robyn hauled ass out the door dressed in a gray pants suit accented with a pink tank top, pink leather flats, and a matching clutch bag in hand. She jumped in her car and tore down City Avenue to I-76. Shockingly, traffic was extremely light. Normally, she would have been in gridlock because of all the construction going on along her route to work. She never understood why the city approved permits for construction work to take place all over the city at the same time. She was convinced there was some evil force working hard to make her commute a living hell.

Robyn stepped off the elevator at 9:45 a.m. She felt she did a damn good job getting to work as quickly as she did. To be able to perform under pressure was one of Robyn's strengths.

As usual, Carolyn greeted Robyn in her typical bubbly voice.

"Hey, honey! Glad to see you made it in okay!"

Robyn was caught a little off guard, but then she remembered she told a lie in order to attempt to keep her ass out of a pot of hot grease.

"Huh? Oh yeah, I'm alright. Thank you, Carol."

Then, in a low whisper, Carol leaned over the desk and said, "I gave Jaycee your message, but if I were you, I'd stay out of her way for a little while. She's acting especially...well, you know..."

Robyn chimed in, "Bitchy?"

Carol blushed and chuckled bashfully like a little schoolgirl. Carol didn't like to say anything bad about anyone. It wasn't in her nature. Good thing for her, Robyn was always around to say out loud in a less than tactful manner whatever Carol may have thought.

Robyn walked over to her desk and sat down. Just as she locked her purse in her desk drawer, Jaycee buzzed her on the intercom.

Robyn took a deep breath and prepared herself for the storm that was about to hit.

"Yes, Jaycee?"

In a cold tone, Jaycee replied, "Robyn, I need to see you in my office...now."

"Okay," Robyn responded. "I'll be right in."

Robyn slowly grabbed her notebook and pen, and walked toward Jaycee's office as if she were on a pirate ship about to walk the plank.

While walking slowly, she said to herself, "Lord, please don't let me have to slap her today."

When Robyn opened the door, Jaycee was sitting at her desk going over some notes.

She glanced up over top of her glasses and said, "Sit down, Robyn."

Robyn sat down and scooted toward the edge of the seat, almost as if preparing for the anticipated slap she was about to lay across Jaycee's face.

There was a short period of awkward silence between the two women before Jaycee began to speak.

"Robyn, this is the third time this week you've been late——"

Robyn cut in. "I know, but——"

Jaycee regained control of the conversation quickly.

"Excuse me, I'm talking now! When I hired you, I clearly explained the importance of you being here on time. I expect you to be in the office and at your desk working by nine o'clock. Not sitting at your desk drinking a cup of coffee or making personal phone calls, but working! Now, if this is too much for you to handle, stop wasting both your time and mine, because you can be replaced.

Robyn felt her jaws tightening as Jaycee continued.

"Now, Robyn, the one thing I cannot and will not tolerate is tardiness! Let this be your official verbal warning. Next time, the incident will be written up and recorded in your personnel file. Is that clear?"

Robyn was fuming, but she managed to keep her attitude professional.

"Yes," she replied.

After her speech, Jaycee acted as if nothing had happened and got right down to business.

"Now, I need you to contact my late afternoon appointments to see if they can either be rescheduled earlier today or tomorrow. Then, I need my quarterly report completed and on my desk by noon and... Robyn, are you writing this down?"

Robyn was still pissed. It was sistahs like Jaycee who were always stepping on another sistah's neck, trying to keep her down. Robyn thought, "*You bitch! Who the fuck do you think you are? Acting all high and mighty like you that bitch that can't be fucked wit'! Then you gonna threaten me? Aww, naw, bitch! It's on! I got something for you...*"

"Robyn...Robyn! Did you hear me?" Jaycee said, annoyed.

Robyn snapped out of her mental tirade. "Huh? Oh, I'm sorry. Would you repeat that, please?"

Jaycee hesitated, sucked her teeth, and then repeated everything she said a second time.

Suddenly, Jaycee blurted out, "Oh, I almost forgot. I'll need you confirm with Ross that we are still on for dinner tonight. Then, make reservations at Davio's for eight o'clock."

Robyn had never heard Jaycee call Ross Daniels by his first name. So, she suspected something was up.

"You mean, Ross...as in Ross Daniels?" Robyn inquired.

"Yes. Do you have a problem with that?" Jaycee asked.

Shaking her head, Robyn uttered, "No."

Robyn knew Jaycee was attracted to Ross, but she didn't think she would ever consider dating him. She knew that went against Jaycee's principles. Usually,

Jaycee was a little more cautious about discussing her personal life. She would have never referred to Ross by his first name in the office. That's how Robyn confirmed something was going on between Jaycee and Ross, whether Jaycee chose to admit or not.

What was more baffling to Robyn was why such a fine specimen of a man like Ross wanted to be bothered with a crab like Jaycee.

Jaycee rolled her eyes and said in a condescending tone, "That will be all. I'm sure you can see yourself out."

Robyn quietly excused herself and returned to her desk. Everything that took place she predicted. If it weren't for the fact that her job was paying for her Master's degree, Robyn would have thrown her notebook in Jaycee's face and told her to kiss her whole ass. She had less than a year to get her piece of paper. Afterwards, she planned to be out and take a few people out with her.

Robyn sat at her desk, her anger brewing. Nevertheless, she laughed it off, picked up the phone, and called Ross to confirm his dinner date with Jaycee. Then, she made another call.

"Good morning. This is Robyn Dalton. I need a huge favor. I need to make arrangements for an extra special dinner for two..."

* * * * *

Four o'clock rolled around, and Jaycee was on her way home to change for her date with Ross. She needed ample time to make sure she looked her best when she saw him. She and Ross had only been dating for a short time. Normally, the whole dating thing would have never been a thought in her mind, especially when it came to clients, which were totally off limits in Jaycee's book. However, Ross was smart, successful, and most of all, fine as hell! Jaycee would have been a fool to let someone like Ross get away.

Jaycee pulled out a brand-new dress that she purchased two weeks before. When she saw it in the window, she instantly fell in love with it. After her shower, she gently slid into a black, sleeveless, rayon mini. Then she put on her high-heeled, leather sandals that were accented with gold links and showed off her beautiful pedicure, and choose to carry a black clutch with the same gold link accents courtesy of Dolce & Gabbana. Her jewelry ensemble consisted of triple-layered gold link earrings and necklace with diamond cuts that gave off a subtle shimmer in the light. Her bobbed hairstyle was pulled behind her ears, giving her a grown and sexy look like Clark, the singer from the movie *Mo' Betta' Blues*. Jaycee's outfit would not have been complete without a little Dolce & Gabbana's Rose The One behind each ear. Her makeup was flawless as if she had it applied professionally at the MAC counter.

Before she walked out the door, Jaycee did a last-minute inspection to make sure nothing was out of place. Her dress hugged her body in all the right places, and her Victoria's Secret bra pushed the twins up to reveal just enough cleavage. Satisfied with how she looked, she grabbed her purse and keys and headed out to meet Ross. She was prepared for the perfect evening and hopefully, a perfect morning.

The Big Payback

Ross got out of his car, walked into the building, and took the elevator up. Somewhat annoyed, he looked at his watch. They had been on several dates, and he still couldn't understand why Jaycee insisted on them driving separate cars. Although her guard was coming down, Jaycee still had a hard time fully trusting anyone. Ross gave up trying to make sense of anything Jaycee did. It was evident to him there was something in her past causing her pain and that she didn't want to let happen again. As long as he had the opportunity to be in the presence of her insurmountable beauty, bask in the sweet smell of her perfume, and anticipate touching her soft skin, Ross would have agreed to just about anything.

When the elevator doors opened, Ross walked down the long, dimly lit corridor. He could smell the scent of Jaycee's perfume as it filled the air. It was the same one she had on during their first encounter. As he got closer, he felt a tingling sensation in his midsection that traveled down into his pants. He followed her scent to a room at the end of the corridor. The door was cracked. He opened the door to find a table in the center of the room. Jazz was playing in the background. Ross loved jazz.

He smiled and thought to himself, *Maybe she was listening when I talked!*

The candles gave off subtle ambient light that was centered on a beautifully table set for two. Ross walked over to the chair, pulled it out, and sat down. There was a bottle of Chianti sitting on the table already opened, so he poured a glass and began to sip slowly while waiting for Jaycee to arrive.

Once again, he smiled while thinking, *Damn, when she said this was going to be a special night to remember, she wasn't playing!*

While Ross sipped his wine and enjoyed the sounds of Branford Marsalis, a shadow began moving toward him from behind. The smell of Jaycee's perfume became stronger. He closed his eyes as his heart started to beat quickly with excitement. Ross was eager to see what awaited him, but he figured since Jaycee went through all the trouble to make this an eventful evening, he would go along with the role-play.

Just as he took another sip of his wine and put the glass on the table, a soft, satin scarf covered his eyes. Then, he felt a scarf being wrapped around his hands. He inhaled the sweet smell of peppermint as she blew seductively in his ear. Ross instantly grew stiff.

He called her name. "Jaycee..."

Before he could get another word out, she put her finger on his mouth and whispered, "Shhhhh..."

She rolled his chair away from the table and walked from behind him. She then took her foot and spread his legs apart to see if he welcomed the treatment he was receiving. She straddled him, creating warm friction as their genitals touched. Ross moaned. Next, her tongue consumed his. Ross tried to reach for her breasts with his mouth, but she pushed him away.

He felt his clothes being slowly undone. His pants and boxers were pulled down toward his ankles. Far be it for him to let her work so hard for something they both wanted. So, he offered a little assistance by raising himself slightly off the chair. He took a deep breath as her tongue ran across every inch of his chocolate body.

In his deep voice, he uttered, "Oh shit! Jaycee, I didn't know you had it like that, girl!"

All of a sudden, Ross felt something warm and wet going up and down on his manhood. His head dropped backward, and his body became limp. Her mouth continued to swallow him from tip to base, in and out, allowing just a little bit of cold air to hit the head in between. Once again, her mouth did a disappearing act and let the tip tickle her tonsils. Just when it appeared that he was about to release, he felt the warm juices from her ocean as she sat and did a slow wine on his rod. Ross wanted so badly to grip her ass as she danced up and down on his shaft. Again, his head made its way toward her breasts, and this time, she let him kiss and lick her nipples. She breathed harder and harder, letting him know he had found her erotic zone. The more she rode, the larger he swelled inside of her. Faster and faster, they moved in unison until Ross was about to burst.

"Jaycee...Oh shit! Damn, baby! You're workin' the shit out of this dick! Get it, baby! Get it all!"

Ross felt her walls tighten, which sent him to a point of no return. Just then, he felt the scarf loosen from his hands, and he grabbed her waist. He felt like something wasn't right, but he was so deep inside her warmth, he couldn't resist.

"Oh shit!" he yelled. "I'm coming, baby! I'm coming!"

Ross let out a growl from deep inside him that could have shook the whole building.

Exhausted, he laughed while trying to catch his breath. "I don't think I have the strength to eat now."

"Awww, too bad. I was just getting warmed up."

Ross paused. He knew then something was very wrong. The voice he heard was not Jaycee's. When she snatched the blindfold off his face, his eyes widened in disbelief.

"What the fuck! Robyn?"

Robyn adjusted her clothes as she laughed at his reaction. "You like my surprise, baby? Umm hmm. Seems to me like you don't know your woman as well as you thought."

Ross grew angry. "You fuckin' bitch! You tricked me!"

Robyn jumped in. "Oh, come on! You can't sit here and tell me that you had no idea you weren't fucking Jaycee. I find that very hard to believe. First of all, have you ever known Jaycee to arrange for you to meet her at the office for dinner? Damn, for someone who has gotten rich from making smart choices, you sure are dumb when it comes to knowing your women. Or is it that maybe you really wanted me instead of her?"

Ross went to reach for Robyn's neck, but she dodged him just in time for him to tip over the chair and fall to the floor. Robyn had also tied his shoelaces to the legs of the chair where only moments ago he sat enjoying himself as her sweet juices ran down his shaft. She reached for a pair of handcuffs she had lying on the floor next to the chair. She had planned to use them for round two of their session. Robyn handcuffed Ross and helped him back onto the chair. If she knew nothing else, she knew she had to find a way to restrain Ross to keep him from choking off her air supply.

"Robyn, get these fuckin' handcuffs off me now! Or so help me, I will..."

"You'll what?" Robyn asked sarcastically. "For the last five years of my life, that bitch has done nothing but make my life here hell. Then, she calls herself threatening to fire folks around here? I couldn't have her fucking up shit for me. She had to pay!" Robyn gave him a seductive look. "You really don't need her. You can have everything your heart desires with me."

Ross looked at Robyn with a look of pity.

"I feel sorry for you. You can't find a good man of your own, so you go out and scam on someone else's. You make me sick!"

Robyn paraded around in front of Ross like a peacock, proud of what she had done. Then she looked at him with an inquisitive expression as she crossed her arms and put her finger on her temple.

"I wonder what Jaycee would say if she found out her man just got finished fucking her assistant? Do you know what that would do to her, especially after she opened herself up to love again after so many years? Tragedy."

Ross looked at Robyn with contempt in his eyes. "Trust and believe, I will tell Jaycee about this. I did nothing wrong. You know your scandalous ass set me up! I'm sure she's seen through your games by now."

"You think?" Robyn asked. "Might I remind you that I've been working under this woman for the last five years? I know more about her than people think I know. Day in and day out, I've watched and learned from the best bitch in the game. You'd be surprised the lengths she would go in order to get ahead, including the late-night, knob-slobbin' sessions with Seth Rothman. People think she has a tough exterior, but I know the truth! She is as transparent as Glad Wrap. Yeah, the shit I've learned from her you definitely don't learn in school, I'll tell you that!"

Robyn moved closer to Ross, opened her wrap dress, and revealed her jewel that had him moaning with pleasure. She took her finger and rubbed her clit. Then, she rubbed her nipples while Ross continued to look on in anger.

"Aww, don't be mad, baby. I just wanted to give you the kind of loving that tight-ass prude could never give you."

Robyn moved in closer as she prepared to go down and suck him off. Ross tried to do whatever he could to push Robyn away. It was as if he were living a nightmare. She managed to get her lips around his manhood and stroke him with precision and care. As much as he tried, Ross couldn't resist Robyn's skill and rose to the occasion. Robyn mounted him yet again and began putting something on Ross that would have him wanting more. This time, Robyn didn't hold back her screams of pleasure. She made sure Ross knew that he felt good to her.

Just as Robyn was about to echo sounds of pleasure, another voice hollered out, "What the fuck is going on here? Ross? Oh, hell naw!"

"Jaycee!" Ross yelled in surprise. "It's not what you think. Baby, please, I can explain everything. I was set up!"

Jaycee didn't know whether to feel angry or hurt. All she knew was this was the straw that broke the camel's back; she was tired. She had opened herself up to love for a third time, just to get the same tired-ass result. A single tear fell from Jaycee's face as she looked into Ross' eyes.

"You happy now?" Jaycee said.

Ross dropped his head in shame, while Robyn just laughed.

"Payback is a motherfucker, isn't it?" Robyn said sarcastically.

Jaycee quickly exchanged her somber look for one of cunningness as she smiled at the both of them.

"Oh, indeed," Jaycee replied.

Jaycee began circling the two of them as she continued. "You see, I pride myself on being the best at what I do. In order to be the best, I have to protect my neck at all times because there is always some young, stupid bitch like you out there trying to take my spot. So, I always have to make sure I'm one step ahead of my competition."

Robyn and Ross watched Jaycee with looks of confusion as she walked over to a cabinet on the wall, which contained a 47-inch flat screen television mounted on the wall. She pulled an object out of her purse that looked like some kind of remote as she continued.

"You know, Robyn, you need to be real careful what you say when you're talking on your business phone. You never know who's listening."

"What the fuck are you talking about, Jaycee?" Robyn asked.

"You mean you've never noticed that your voice echoes whenever you're being recorded? Maybe you're not as smart as I thought you were."

Robyn's eyes lit up in surprise as she suddenly heard her voice coming across a small digital recorder that Jaycee was holding in her hand. It was the conversations she had with the caterers who she paid using Jaycee's corporate credit card to set up dinner in the conference room, and Robyn letting Ross know that instead of meeting at Davio's, he was to meet Jaycee at the office.

Jaycee laughed and then quickly shifted her attention to Ross while still addressing Robyn.

"I have to give it to you, Robyn. You were right about one thing. For Ross to be so successful and smart with his business practices, he certainly is dumb when it comes to his women."

Jaycee reached for another remote that sat on a desk next to a computer. On the wall next to the computer hung a black, wireless camera. She turned on the television, and both Robyn and Ross' eyes grew wide with surprise. On the screen played the fuck session that occurred moments before Jaycee walked in. It took everything Jaycee had to control herself from whipping Robyn's ass as she watched the event for the second time.

"You bitch!" Robyn yelled.

Jaycee turned to Robyn and said, "Yeah, and this bitch has been on to you since you walked in these fuckin' doors. I remotely accessed a live feed from this room and watched the festivities from my cell phone."

Robyn was unsure if the feed was still streaming. She didn't want to be caught on camera catching a case for trying to kill Jaycee.

" A little bit of advice, Robyn. Next time, make sure you survey your surroundings before you try settin' bitches up to take a fall," Jaycee said.

Jaycee had found out about Robyn's plan, and she quickly sprung into attack mode. After Robyn left the office to put the finishing touches on her plan, Jaycee put her plan into motion. She set up video surveillance to stream not only to the partners' computers, but to the computer of Jerry Jones, a news reporter whom she met at a networking function a few years ago. Jaycee cleaned out her office of all her personal belongings and wiped her computer clean of all her client files and emails. After leaving the office, she went to a payphone right outside the office building and made a call.

Feeling helpless, Ross pleaded, "Baby, I'm telling you that she set me——"

Jaycee quickly regained control of the conversation. "Shut the fuck up, you grimy bastard! I'm talking now. As much mileage that this bitch has on her tired-ass pussy, you couldn't tell the difference between her and me? As fast as your dick disappeared between her legs, you should have known it wasn't me! I sat outside in my car and waited to see if you would get a fuckin' clue. I watched your body respond to hers in the same way it did to mine. Not to mention, you fucked this bitch with no protection. I'm sure the two of you will be very happy together, because rest assured, your dick will never feel the walls of this pussy again!"

On her way out the door, Jaycee threw a piece of paper on Ross' lap as he sat there with his pants still around his ankles. It was confirmation of a wire transfer in the sum of five million dollars from his personal bank account to an undisclosed account. Ross' eyes turned the color of fire.

Jaycee looked over her shoulder, laughing. "Just a little reparations for my pain and suffering."

She walked toward Robyn, smiled, and dropped her like a bad habit with a nice jab combination to her jaw and eye. Then, she fixed her hair and adjusted her boobs, and while Robyn lie on the floor, she told her, "Another word of advice. A guppy never survives swimming around in shark infested waters."

Next, Jaycee looked at her watch and said, "Will you look at the time? I've got to go. The news will be coming on soon."

Ross sat there as he watched her sexy ass switch back and forth underneath her dress.

Jaycee walked down the hall of RSM Investment Group for the last time. She took the service elevator down to the ground floor and exited out of a side door. When Jaycee reached the corner of the block, she looked toward the entrance of the building to see news trucks loitering outside. As she headed to her car, she walked past an electronics store that had televisions in the window playing the video footage she had captured on the ten o'clock news. The news headline read, *RSM INVESTMENT GROUP PROSTITUTION SCANDAL! USE OF CORPORATE VIXENS TO INCREASE CLIENTELE.*

Jaycee laughed her ass off as she watched her handiwork at its finest. As she headed to her car, she thought, *This shit would make a great book!*

VENDETTA

T. Real

Chapter 1

Monique Wright raced towards the front door of Jackson Studios like a rabbit running from its prey. The white blouse she wore to the casting call had been torn during the struggle to fight off her attacker. Despite being in a frantic state, she was still able to think on her feet while running to the corner where her car was parked.

She hopped inside her vehicle, but because she was so hysterical, she couldn't drive. Her hands were shaking like a dopefiend going through withdrawal. Knowing the tears streaming from her eyes would ruin her makeup, Monique reached in the glove compartment to grab a few tissues, then flipped down the mirror on the sun visor and proceeded to wipe her face. As she wiped away the streaked cosmetics from her caramel complexion, she used the breathing technique she had learned in her yoga class to help calm her down. The technique worked like a charm; however, it did nothing to erase her memory of being felt up by Randy Martin of Randy Martin Productions, the perverted producer who was still inside the studio with sore genitalia.

Revisiting the event that had just taken place only moments ago made her disgusted again as she pushed the ignition button to start her 2011 Burgundy Lacrosse. As she drove up the one-way street, Randy exited the building and looked around to see where she had gone. While driving past him, she stuck up her middle finger and then made a left, making her way towards home.

Monique was an accomplished actress who had starred in commercials, plays, and even a couple of independent films that received local accolades. She was well paid because she hustled. When not acting, she worked temp jobs at local agencies to keep the cash flowing, but acting was her passion. Since she possessed the height and flawless features, she even did a little modeling on the side. Her drive to be successful resulted in her being sought out by many production companies in the city. However, due to what had just taken place, Randy Martin Productions was one company she would never return to for work.

* * * * *

Monique kicked off her heels and headed straight to the living room after entering her house. Feeling the need to relax, she sat in the reclining section of her plush leather couch. Kicking back helped her body, but her mind was still flooded with thoughts.

What should I do? Who should I call? Should I call the cops and report the incident?

Having never been in a situation like this before, and not knowing anyone who had been, she was left feeling confused on how to handle it. She decided to pour herself a glass of wine, hoping to clear her mind. She guzzled the first glass and then poured another. While taking a sip from the second drink, her phone began to ring. The number displayed on her screen wasn't stored in her phone, so she didn't answer it. Instead, she placed her phone on the coffee table and took another sip of wine. Not a minute later, she received a call from the same number. This time, she exhaled and directed the call to her voicemail.

"This is not the time for prank calls or someone calling with the wrong number," Monique said out loud before sipping from her glass once more.

As soon as she put down the glass, her phone rang again. Her patience having grown thin from the same person continuously calling, she decided to answer.

"Hello," Monique answered, irritation deeply rooted in her voice.

When the caller didn't say anything, it only made Monique more agitated.

"Look, I'm too grown for childish games. Play on somebody else's phone, or go..."

Before she could finish her rant, the caller spoke.

"I'm sorry."

"You're sorry? First, acknowledge who you are."

"It's Randy."

"Look, you're the last person I want to speak to right now."

"I know, and you have every right to be upset after what happened tonight. Things should have never gone down like that. I'm calling for another chance."

"Another chance?! Please! Good luck with finding another actress with my skills," Monique shouted into the phone's receiver, speaking through her pain with confidence.

"I know I was out of line, but I got beside myself. I actually thought you wanted it, just like I did."

"Well, you thought wrong!" Monique yelled.

When she finished expressing herself, a sharp pain pierced through her forehead. Her body began to overheat, and beads of sweat seeped from the pores of her skin.

"How can I make it up to you?" Randy asked. "This is the first time this has ever happened to me."

"Yeah, right! I'm quite sure you did this before, you pervert. Look, just leave me the hell alone!" Monique yelled.

Another pain shot through her forehead. This time, the pain brought on much more. She began sniffing what she thought was clear fluid coming out of her nose.

"Look, you whore..."

"Whore?! Who you calling a whore? You're lucky I don't come find you right now and cut off that little thing between your legs you call a penis," Monique said before hanging up.

As she sat the phone down, she noticed blood on her hand and panicked as she made her way to the bathroom, tripping over the rug on her way. Finally making it to the sink, she washed her hands and face. While doing so, she looked in the mirror and was disgusted with her reflection. He face looked like she had been in a sparing match. There was smeared blood above her top lip, and her eyes were beginning to form bags under them as if she hadn't slept in days.

After a hot bath, I'll be back to normal, she thought to herself, while turning on the faucet to run some bath water.

As the tub filled, she took off her remaining garments, wrapped herself in a towel, and returned to the living room to finish her glass of wine. She wanted a third glass, but decided to wait until after her bath. On her way back to the bathroom to turn off the water, she was stopped in her tracks when her phone started to ring for the fourth time. She picked up her cell phone to see who was calling this time. In the back of her mind, she wanted it to be Randy again so she could cuss him out once more, but it wasn't him. It was Johan, a bald-headed, tall, dark love interest.

She looked at Johan as a potential husband. Her attraction to him was simply that she had a love jones for wealthy, dark-complexioned, bald men. Her favorite dark-skinned man was Michael Jordan, but since he was unattainable, she settled for Johan. She would even joke and tell him that, but Johan didn't find it funny.

Along with Johan's good looks came a fat wallet since he owned his own line of suits and a boutique on South Street. That's where the two of them met one day while Monique was shopping, and they had been dating ever since.

Monique took a deep breath before answering, trying to suppress her crazy day in a matter of seconds.

"Hey, Johan," she answered, still coming off a little dry.

"What's up, sexy? Sounds like you had a long day."

Monique exhaled. "You have no idea."

"Did I catch you at a bad time?"

"No. I was just about to soak in the tub, that's all," she told him as she walked into the bathroom and turned off the faucet just in time to keep the bathtub from overflowing.

"In that case, can I come join you?"

"As good as that sounds right now, Johan, I'll have to take a rain check until tomorrow. Sorry."

"Oh okay. So that means we're still on for dinner at your house?" he asked.

"Yes, and what are you cooking?"

Johan chuckled before replying, "I'll surprise you."

"Sounds good. Can't wait."

Johan was a great cook, which was another quality Monique liked about him.

"I'm taking care of everything," he added. "All you have to do is be sexy."

Monique blushed. "Now you know I have no problem doing that. What time are you coming?"

"Between seven and eight o'clock. Sometime after I close the store."

"Sounds good. Well, let me go so I can enjoy this bath and unwind," Monique told him.

"Okay, but let me warn you. If you see a fly on the wall, that's me," Johan said, causing Monique to burst into laughter.

"You're so crazy. I needed that laugh. Thank you."

"You're welcome," Johan responded before hanging up.

Monique took off her towel and hung it on the rack next to the tub. She then stuck her foot in the water to test the temperature. It was nice and hot just the way she liked her baths. So, she got all the way in. After soaking for about five minutes, her mind drifted back to what took place at the studio. Facts started to pop into her head as she played detective.

Randy Martin has his own studio, so why did he do the audition at Jackson Studios, and why was I the only one there?

She started to feel like she had been a target, and if it happened to her, it could happen to another female of her status. Or maybe it had already happened.

In the midst of all the thinking, she felt her eyes getting heavy and her head nodding, so she grabbed for the washcloth and soap. After lathering up her body, she rinsed off and let the water out. She grabbed the towel off the rack, wrapped it around her wet body, and walked over to the sink. After wiping away the condensation from the mirror, making a small shrieking sound in the process as her hand rubbed across the glass, she applied toothpaste to her toothbrush and began brushing her teeth. After two minutes of brushing, she reached into the medicine cabinet and grabbed the mouthwash. While gargling, her phone rang.

Great. Perfect timing, she thought, being sarcastic with herself as she bent over to spit out the mouthwash.

As she rose up and looked at the mirror, she saw the figure of a man coming towards her from behind. Quickly spinning around, she noticed it was Randy with his arms stretched out, coming for her neck.

Monique let out a loud scream, waking herself up from the brief nightmare and causing a splash in the bath. She hadn't realized she had fallen asleep. She looked around astonished at first, before wiping off her hand so she could answer her ringing phone.

"Hey, Mom."

"About time you answered. What took you so long?" her mother asked.

"I was taking a bath and ended up dosing off."

"How many times have I told you to stop taking baths when you're tired?"

"Yeah, yeah, Mom, I know. I could drown."

"Okay. Well, since you've learned your lesson for the day, let's move on to why I'm calling. I called to see about us spending some mother/daughter time tomorrow. I made us reservations at a spa, and we can do brunch."

"Wow, Mom, and what if I said no? How about a heads up before time and not at the last minute?"

"Sorry. I just wanted to surprise you and take you out 'cause I know you got that part."

Silence fell upon the conversation.

"Hello. I know you got that part, right?"

"Mom, I'll tell you all about it tomorrow. Let me go so I can finish up my bath and get some rest."

Right after Monique hung up, she laid back in the bath, put her hands over her face, and began sobbing. She didn't want to have to tell her mother, but she knew she had no choice now. And God forbid if her mother told her father what happened.

After crying for several minutes, she took a couple of deep breaths and remembered why she had taken a bath in the first place––to relax.

Upon getting out of the tub, she brushed her teeth, gargled with some mouthwash, and then proceeded to her room, where she laid on her back across the bed and stared at the ceiling. Her mind raced with thoughts, but the only thing she wanted to do before drifting off to sleep was to dream about something happy instead of the nightmare that had just taken place a couple of hours prior.

Chapter 2

Feeling refreshed, Monique woke up yawning and stretching at the same time. She grabbed her cell phone and saw she had three missed calls and a message. Just from looking at the time, she knew who the missed calls were from and quickly dialed the number.

"Uh huh. Look who decided to finally wake up. I called you three times and even left a text message."

"Sorry for oversleeping, Mom."

"You're lucky I could reschedule, or you would be paying me what I put down."

"Okay, Mom, I said I was sorry. Now where are we going to eat brunch?

"I made reservations to go to Newtown Grille for 11am. "Well, let me get myself together, and I will meet you there."

"And please, baby, don't be late."

"Okay, Mom. Sheesh!"

After hanging up, Monique got up to relieve herself, took a quick shower, and got dressed. Not wanting to overdress, she decided she would look presentable in an all-white shirt that displayed a hint of her cleavage, a pair of black tights, and her favorite heels that had studs on the front.

Once dressed, she brushed her hair into a bun and rushed out the door.

* * * * *

Monique pulled up to Newtown Grille. As she entered she spotted her mother arms folded, due to her mannerisms Monique knew she was going to receive some type of attitude. But she greeted her with a hug and smile but that still wasn't enough.

"Well, I guess fifteen minutes isn't that bad."

"Please, I made it. Now give me a break, Lillian", Monique shouted playfully. She only used her mother's government when she wanted to shut her down.

"Now we have to wait for the hostess since I told her that I was waiting for you."

Just as Lillian was done speaking the hostess walked up to greet them. "Welcome to Newtown Grille may I help you?" She said in a perky voice.

Monique's mother enjoyed the hospitality and read her name tag before answering.

"Thank you Kelly, reservations for the Wrights please".

Kelly typed into her system and brought up their reservation.

"Lillian Wright", she asked with courtesy.

"Yes", Lillian answered with a smile.

"Ok, to my right is the buffet. And behind the buffet is the dining area." She paused as she reached her hand out for a demonstration. "Since it's not crowded it's your choice of where to sit. Please be seated and I will be with you shortly to take your drink order .

"Thanks Kelly", Lillian said as they proceed pass the buffet to sit down.

While walking pass Monique noticed an elderly couples sitting down indulging in conversation and another on the other side of the room.

"Mom, I know you don't have me up in no Nursing Home".

"Monique", Lillian said appalled at her daughter's comment. "No this is not a nursing home why would I take you to eat at a nursing home? A dear friend of mine recommended this place and she said the food is delicious."

"It does smell good" Monique said as they sat down.

After sitting down Monique and Lillian looked over their silverware. As they were done Monique's stomach began growling. She looked at her motherwith wide eyes and her head cocked to the side.

"Look mom I don't know about you but I'm hungry and I'm going to get my food now. If the hostess comes back, order me a Mimosa".

Monique walked over to the buffet and scoured over the selections. So much food overwhelmed her. She decided to start off small with pancakes, eggs, sausage, honey dew and cantaloupe. After getting her food she walked back to where they were seated. Lillian could read her like an open book. From the look on her daughter's face and the way she exhaled when she sat down Lillian knew that something was wrong. After letting her say her grace Lillian spoke.

"Sorry if this place isn't jammed packed with a DJ booth." Lillian said sarcastically.

"Mom it's not that bad, Monique answered back while cutting up her pancakes. Why don't you go get you something to eat then we can converse when you get back. Lillian reluctantly left the area and headed toward the buffet tables.

Lillian arrived back in ten minutes sat down prayed and began eating her asparagus, honey dew and watermelon. Monique started to get uncomfortable with the silence so she broke the ice.

"So how's Dad?" Monique asked.

"He's great, despite one situation." Lillian answered

"What is it? I hope nothing too serious." Monique said becoming instantly concerned about her father.

"He's been diagnosed with erectile dysfunction."

"Too much information, Mom. I don't need to hear about my dad in that way." Monique said as she put her fork down and sat back folding her arms feeling like she was about to lose her appetite.

Lillian questioned her daughter's actions.

"I thought you were hungry", Lillian asked in between bites of fruit.

"Yeah and you almost made me lose my appetite, but I'm cool now" Monique said as she picked up her fork again stabbing into her pancakes.

"Well, you asked." Lillian said shrugging her shoulders

"And you would be the one to tell me, right?" Monique said shaking her head.

"Okay, well, let's change the subject. How's your love life?" Lillian asked as she leaned in close waiting for an answer.

Monique paused for a second before answering. "It's good. Me and Johan are still dating."

"Your hesitation makes me think otherwise." Lillian said.

"It's just that we didn't make it official that we're a couple yet, and that's what I want." Monique said becoming a little emotional.

"Well, let me be the first to tell you that he might be seeing someone else. I caught him flirting with some bimbo inside his boutique," Lillian informed her. "I even got a picture of her."

Lillian reached into her purse and pulled out her cellphone. After scrolling through her phone to find the picture she showed Monique. Monique leaned in and just shook her head while looking at the picture.

"How did you manage to do that? Monique asked.

Lillian smiled proudly and gave an account of how savvy she was.

"I asked her what type of weave she was wearing. Then I acted like I liked it so much that I had to take a picture of it to show my hairdresser."

Monique folded her arms trying to contain her emotions.

"When did all this take place? And why are you just now telling me mom?"

After taking a sip of her drink Lillian continued.

"It was like a week ago. I stopped past Johan's store to pick up some suits for your dad while I was out running errands. And I didn't tell you sooner because I wanted you to be focused on your audition. Speaking of your audition, you didn't sound too excited after I asked how it went. So, share all the details." Lillian said changing the subject.

Monique took a deep breath, and right before she was about to explain what had happened, the server approached the table with their Mimosas, interrupting her. After thanking the server, Lillian took a sip and then looked at Monique as if waiting for her to continue.

"Mom, before I go into details, please promise me you won't tell Dad."

"Why? What happened? Let me guess. You performed a sexual favor and still struck out."

"Mom!" Monique yelled, and then lowered her voice, not wanting to cause a scene. It was too late to cause a scene since every senior's eyes were looking in their direction. Monique wasn't even paying attention to them she just kept on conversing.

"No, Mom. What type of actress do you take me for, one with no talent? I was assaulted last night. The producer tried to rape me." Monique said lowering her voice

"And you didn't call the cops? Take me over there right now," Monique's mother said, while standing up and pulling out a taser from her purse.

"Mom, sit down and put that away. I was in shock and confused as to why it even happened. So, no, I didn't call the cops. And don't you know that pervert had the nerve to call and apologize to me right after."

"No, he didn't. That's why we need to go to where he's at right now and teach him a lesson."

Monique reached out stopped her mom from rising again.

"Calm down, Mom. Remember, we're in public. You know what, though? I'm not going to let what happened discourage me from pursuing my dreams. I have another audition coming up, plus a networking party to attend."

"Well, I'm glad you have a strong spirit and not letting this one incident break you."

"Thanks for the support, Mom, and remember, don't tell Dad."

"I'm not. I'm not. I promise."

Monique and her mother continued conversing over two more glasses of Mimosa while enjoying their brunch. Once they finished eating, and as they were heading out the door, Monique received a text message. The ringtone, Miguel's "All I Want is You", alerted her as to who had sent the message. She pulled out her phone and read the text, which brought a huge smile to her face. Observant, her mother wanted to know why she was grinning so hard.

"Did we receive some good news?" she asked with a hint of sarcasm.

"No, *we* didn't receive any good news, but it looks as though *I* did. Might turn out to be a good night."

"Oh, that can only mean that you're going to be in the company of Johan. Just make sure you get to the bottom of that business I told you about regarding that other woman."

"I'm glad you said something," Monique said "Make sure you text me that picture."

"No problem. Now give me a hug, and call me if you need anything."

Monique gave her mother a hug, and then they departed from each other's company.

As soon as Monique pushed the button to start her car, her phone went off, signaling she had received a text. She stared at the picture for a minute, looking at the smile on the culprit's face. If she were to come across the person in the picture right at that moment, she would have ripped her a part limb by limb.

She quickly dismissed the thoughts and focused her mind on the dinner date she was about to have with Johan. She wanted the time with him to be centered on them being happy.

* * * * *

During the ride home, Monique pondered on what she would wear, how she would style her hair, and if she was going to wear any makeup. She was happy that she would have time to clean up and even take a nap before Johan arrived.

When she entered her home, she sighed at the relief of not having much to clean up. After a quick inspection, she decided the only things she needed to do was vacuum, wipe off the tables and counters, and straighten up her room. Before starting, she put on Mary J. Blige's *No More Drama* CD. Then she began in her bedroom by changing her sheets and vacuuming. Once she finished in the bedroom, she vacuumed from the hallway and into the living room/dining room area. Dancing and singing along to the songs, she proceeded to the kitchen to wash the few dishes that were in the sink and wipe down the counters. Afterwards, she placed scented candles in her living room and bedroom.

By the time the CD ended, the cleaning was complete. She glanced at the time and saw it was 3:30 p.m., which left Monique close to two and a half hours before she needed to start getting ready for Johan's arrival. So, she decided to lie down and take a nap to reenergize herself.

Before lying down, she grabbed her laptop to check her emails and Facebook page. After shifting her pillows to get comfortable, she lied down, logged on to her Facebook and Google email accounts, then began browsing and clicking. One email that caught her attention was an email blast from Randy that stated he would announce which actress would be awarded the lead role in his film on Facebook at eight o'clock that evening. Sure that she wouldn't get the part after what had happened, Monique clicked on two other events that she was attending, one casting call and an actresses networking event, to make sure the time and dates had not changed. Then she logged off. Yawning, Monique closed her laptop, set her phone's alarm for six o'clock, and then closed her eyes to enjoy her catnap.

What seemed like only minutes later, Monique's alarm chimed, waking her. After silencing the alarm, she saw she had an unread text message from Johan stating he would be arriving between seven and seven-thirty. Once she read the message, she stretched, hopped out of bed, and went into her closet to pull out her all-purpose black dress and black flats. She placed the dress on the bed before going into the bathroom to run her bath water, adding some milk bubble bath to it.

After soaking for about fifteen minutes, she got out, dried off, and applied some Bath & Body Works Vanilla Sugar scented lotion to her body. While applying the lotion, she thought about how she was going to style her hair. She decided to just let her hair flow down her back. Johan always complimented her on how sexy she looked every time she wore it that way.

Once she finished flat-ironing her hair, she got dressed and then took a look in the mirror, admiring her sexiness from all angles. When her phone rang, she thought it was Johan calling, but it was her mother.

"Hello, Mom. Monique said while rolling her eyes

"How's your date so far?" Lillian asked.

"It didn't even start yet, I just finished getting dressed.", Monique replied while still admiring herself in the mirror.

"Okay, good. So Johan is not around. I was just calling to remind you to make sure you ask him about Ms. Anonymous."

"Don't worry, Mom. I'll ask him, and please don't call for the rest of the night because I'll be busy." Monique said in a demanding way.

Lillian pulled the phone away from here not believing what she just heard. She wanted to ask who she was talking to but she decided to let it go and went back to conversing. "I'm sure you will be. Well, just call and let me know what's what."

"Okay, Mom," Monique said as she walked into the bathroom to retrieve her favorite lip-gloss. She blew her a kiss before hanging up.

Monique shook her head and chuckled. She knew her mother had her best interest at heart, but she could be too nosy at times.

After their brief conversation, Monique checked the time. It was 6:50 p.m., and Johan would soon be arriving. So, to set the mood, she lit each candle she had in place and dimmed the lamps. The next time her phone rang, it was Johan. At the exact same time, the sound of his Porsche Panorama could be heard entering her driveway. Instead of answering the phone, she walked to the door to greet him. As he got out his car, he grabbed the grocery bags and walked inside.

"Let me put these bags down so I can properly greet you," he told her.

Monique didn't respond; she stood there speechless while watching his every move as he placed the bags on the counter. She could feel herself getting slightly moist between her thighs, anticipating their bodies coming together.

"Now that those bags are out of the way, come here," Johan said in an aggressive manner.

Following his command, Monique pranced over and pressed herself against his chest. The caressing of their bodies caused her to experience a warm sensation throughout her body as she smiled and exhaled.

"You smell good," Johan complimented as their bodies separated from each other's tight grasp.

"Thanks. I'm trying out this new fragrance. I'm glad you like it. And you don't smell bad yaself."

"Thanks." Johan took a step back to get a clear view of Monique's ensemble. "Whoo! You're wearing the hell out of that dress, and you know how much I love it when you wear your hair like that."

Monique blushed and then asked him about the food.

"So what are you cooking?"

"I'm going to fix steak, my special home fries with sautéed onions and green peppers, and a salad. Plus, I brought some wine to top it off."

"Yum! Sounds good. And for dessert?"

"You," Johan answered with a devilish grin, making Monique blush and chuckle.

"You so nasty," Monique stated, while going closer to Johan and planting her moist lips on his. "Okay, enough kissing. If we keep it up, there won't be any food getting cooked," she said, pushing Johan away so he could start the food preparation.

Monique's phone chimed again, alerting her that it was eight o'clock. Leaving Johan to cook, she went into her bedroom and grabbed her laptop to entertain herself. As she sat down and opened the laptop, a nervous spell came over her. Praying that she still had a chance, she grew nervous from the anticipation of who was going to be named the leading lady in Randy's production of *Diva*.

When Monique logged on, she went straight to Randy's Facebook page to see the announcement. Her jaw dropped as she looked at the picture and status. She grabbed her cell phone and retrieved the photo her mother had sent her earlier. The people in both photos were identical. Now she had a name to put with the face that went along with her mother's story. The woman's name was Erica Banks.

Monique began feeling numb inside. She felt that role would have been perfect for her, and the feeling of having it stolen from her quickly sunk in. Things weren't adding up. She got assaulted, and then the anonymous woman caught flirting with Johan by her mother is the same one who got the part. Johan broke her deep thoughts when he gently kissed her on the neck.

"Now that everything is simmering and baking, I wanted to take a quick break. What you doing?"

"Nothing, just browsing on Facebook."

Johan glanced at the picture and recognized Erica.

"Hey, I know her. As a matter of fact, that suit she has on in that picture is from my store."

"Wait. When did you start selling women's suits?"

"I would say about two weeks ago."

"Oh, so you sold her a suit? Did you give her anything else?" Monique questioned, like she was interrogating him.

"No, and why am I getting the third degree regarding somebody who I only met once?"

Before she could answer, Johan read the post. Putting two and two together, he realized why Monique's mood had suddenly changed. He tried to console her by kissing her on the neck again, but she backed away.

"Don't try and butter me up. What happened when the bitch came into your store?"

"Nothing. She was very professional. All she wanted was a suit. Then your mother came in and took her picture, saying something about how much she liked her hair."

"And that's all that happened?" Monique said, sounding as if she doubted he was telling her the whole story. "What type of conversation did y'all have before my mom walked in?"

"She only wanted to know how long I had been in business. I simply took her measurements, and because of how professional I was, she said she would bring a lot more business my way."

"I bet you enjoyed that."

"Hell yeah! The more customers the better, right? That's how I stay in business."

"Very funny. I was talking about you measuring her."

"I didn't enjoy it as much as I like to measure you," Johan said as he caressed her 34-D breasts.

Monique giggled and turned to kiss Johan.

"I'm hungry. When is the food going to be done?"

"Let me whip up this salad and set the table. By the time I finish, dinner should be ready."

Johan set the mood to perfection. He prepared their plates, poured the champagne, lit some dinner candles, and put on a mix CD of appropriate slow jams. The Isley Brothers' "Let Me Know" started played low enough so they could hear each other while conversing over dinner.

Monique was there physically, but mentally, her mind was on the Erica Banks character. She was over the fact about Erica possibly flirting with Johan. Her mind was getting bent out of shape thinking about how Erica had gotten the part instead of her. It started to become obvious to Johan that Monique wasn't all there. She was even eating slow while staring off into space.

"Monique," Johan said, calling her name to get her attention.

"Huh? Oh, I'm sorry, babe. The food is good."

"I didn't ask you how the food tasted. I just called your name. What's wrong? You're not here with me one hundred percent. I can tell something is on your mind."

"I know, and I'm sorry if I'm ruining this perfect night, but I can't keep my mind off how that bitch got my part."

"Don't worry so much. Look at it like this. You win some and you lose some."

Monique didn't like how Johan responded. So, she just sipped her champagne and didn't respond. His directness was like adding more fuel to a fire.

Sensing Monique had an attitude with the way he had replied, he said, "Let me ask you this. Why is it so important for you to know?"

"'Cause I feel like she stole the part and didn't work hard for it. But, you know what? You're right. Why am I tripping? I got two events to attend, and I'm sure I'll find out something. The industry is always buzzing with gossip."

"Well, if you're gonna go around digging, make sure you don't get yourself caught up or even blackballed."

"Trust me, I will not get caught. I'm going to find out what I need to know without snooping around."

Monique sighed, signaling to Johan that she was still a little stressed out. As he looked across the table at her, she picked at the scraps of food on her plate with her fork. He rose from his seat, walked over to stand behind her, then started massaging her shoulders and neck. His actions were right on time as R Kelly's "12-Play" began to play.

Being the romantic he was, Johan whispered in her ear, "What do you say we take this into the bedroom?"

Monique giggled as goose bumps covered her body from how sexy his voice sounded in her ear.

"I don't feel like walking. How about you carry me?"

"No problem," Johan said, then picked her up and carried her all the way to the bedroom, where he laid her gently on the bed.

He slipped her out of her dress, removed her panties, and rolled her on to her stomach. He then stripped down until he was naked himself. Monique told him to grab the massage oil from off her dresser. Following her orders, he grabbed the sensual oil that smelled like cinnamon.

"Oh, and don't use too much. It's the kind that gets hot when you start rubbing," Monique told him.

Keeping that in mind, Johan squirted a small amount into the palm of his hand and then applied it to her back. Monique moaned from the pleasurable feel of Johan's masculine hands. After massaging her back for five minutes, he eased down to her legs and feet. Wanting to cover every inch of her body, Johan flipped her onto her back. He squirted more oil into his hand before he started massaging her breasts.

Monique slowly took hold of his penis and began massaging him until he was fully erect. As she stroked him, Johan inserted his fingers inside her welcoming inner walls, and when he removed them, they were drenched from her juices. Unable to contain himself any longer, Johan maneuvered himself on top of Monique and then slid his penis deep inside her until she moaned and clawed at his back. He grinded inside her until he felt her walls grip tighter around his penis and she yelled out his name while climaxing.

After twenty minutes of hard lovemaking, Johan climaxed, and they both fell asleep in a spooning position. It was exactly what Monique needed to take her away from the reality she faced. However, she couldn't escape the nightmare that invaded her mind as soon as she fell asleep.

* * * * *

Monique entered Jackson Studios full of confidence and excited about being casted for the lead role in a Randy Martin Production called *Diva*. She didn't even pay attention to the fact that she was the only one there auditioning. Her mind was strictly on handling her business and landing the part. As she made it to Stage 3, she made her presence known.

"Hello!" Monique said, her voice echoing off the walls.

"Hello. My name is Randy Martin, and I'll be conducting the casting call. Here's the script. All you have to do is memorize your part, and I will read as the other character from the paper. I will give you about ten minutes to rehearse while I take care of some paperwork. If you need more time, just let me know."

Too busy reading the script, Monique didn't notice Randy eye balling her, admiring her every curve.

"No. Ten minutes is just fine."

"Great. Well, let me finish up taking care of what I was doing, and I'll be right back out," Randy said before walking away.

With her being a veteran, Monique was able to memorize what was needed with no problem.

"So how's everything going? You need more time to get into character?" Randy asked when he returned.

"No, I'm ready," she responded.

Randy grabbed his script and sat down at the desk he used as a prop in the scene. Monique stepped off the stage, and then at the request of Randy, the scene was ready to be acted out.

"And action!" Randy blurted out.

Monique walked on stage in a seductive manner as the sound of her heels echoed off the walls.

"Working hard or hardly working?" Monique recited.

"Oh, you have no idea," Randy said, reading from the script. "I've had a long day. So what brings you here?"

"I want to take you up on that offer you had on the table," Monique said as she sat on the desk and crossed her legs, showing some thigh through the split of her skirt as she got deeper into character.

"So what made you change your mind? I mean, just yesterday you stormed out of my office," Randy said, while getting up and walking around the desk to where Monique was now leaning back on her elbows on the desk.

He placed his hand on her thigh and caressed it. Monique went along with it, thinking it was written in the scene that way. By the time she went to follow up with her lines, he had both hands on her hips and was pulling her closer for a kiss.

"That's not in the script!" she blurted out.

"I know. This is what they call improvising."

Monique tried to squirm out of his grasp, but the more she squirmed the tighter he gripped her. As she fought off Randy in the nightmare, she thrashed about in the arms of Johan.

"Stop!" she screamed, waking Johan.

As she woke up in darkness, she started to attack Johan, slapping him and trying to get out of the arms she had fallen asleep in.

"Monique! Monique! It's me. You were dreaming," Johan said.

They were both now on the floor, having fell off the bed as he tried to calm her down.

"I'm sorry, Johan. I had a crazy nightmare," Monique said, while trying to compose herself and steady her breathing.

"Let me go get you some water while you get yourself together."

When Johan came back with a glass of water, Monique was sitting on the edge of the bed staring out of the window as the moonlight illuminated the night sky. After handing her the water, Johan started rubbing her back gently.

"Are you okay now?"

"Yes, I'm good. Let me finish drinking this water, and I'll be back to sleep".

Johan kissed her on the cheek and then laid down. While Monique sipped the water and stared out the window, she tried to think of how she could shake the incident from her thoughts. It was starting to haunt her in her dreams now, and the one thing she didn't need was for it to interfere with what she was trying to accomplish. As she snuggled up against Johan, she silently prayed that she would be successful with the business she had to handle the next day. A few minutes later, she had fallen back to sleep.

Chapter 3

Full of confidence, Monique entered the Holiday Inn. Her spirit had her feeling untouchable, even in spite of her nightmare last night. All she had on her mind was handling her business like she always did. She read the sign stating where the casting call was being held, took an elevator down to the ballroom area, and walked until she came up on fifteen other women who were standing in line. Reading the sign, she knew she was in the right place. Just as she read on the event page online, it was an audition for a commercial. A new adult phone service was being birthed, and they were filming a commercial. A lady sitting at a desk to the right of the sign stood up, greeted Monique, and handed her two pieces of paper and a pen.

"Hello, this is the script you have to memorize, and the other one paper is for you to leave all your contact information in lieu of you being selected for the part."

"Thank you," Monique responded, then started to fill out the paperwork.

After completing the sheet, she gave it back to the lady at the desk and got right down to business of memorizing the script. As she walked away to find a nice quiet spot, one of the women in line approached her, introducing herself.

"Hello, my name is Angel. And you are?"

"Nice to meet you, Angel. I'm Monique."

Angel came off very friendly and outgoing, but Monique really didn't like to brown nose with what she deemed her competition. But, since she didn't want to come off as being conceited, she greeted Angel as she had been greeted.

"Well, it was good meeting you, Monique. Just wanted to say good luck to you today."

"Thanks, and the same to you," Monique responded before she walked away.

While walking, a female who was coming down the hallway caught her attention. Monique had never questioned her sexuality before, but she couldn't take her eyes off this one. The woman's hair bounced with each step she took., and her outfit fit every curve of her body to perfection. Her makeup, which was flawless, made her brown sugar complexion shine like diamonds in the sun.

With the female possessing such attributes, Monique knew she would be her competition for the day.

After finding a nice spot behind the six-foot beauty where she could memorize the lines, Monique still found herself distracted. She couldn't help herself; she had to know who the woman was.

"Excuse me, I'm not pushing up on you or anything. I just wanted to let you know you're wearing that skirt."

"Thank you. That means a lot coming from you, Monique."

"Oh, so you know who I am?" Monique said surprised raising her eyebrows.

"Of course. You're my inspiration, even though you've succeeded in landing every big part I've ever tried out for during my career."

"Well, I'm touched to hear I'm your inspiration, and I hope you don't take my ambition personal."

"I never took it personal. You just made me never give up."

Monique felt great having finally met someone who she had inspired, especially someone that didn't turn their nose up at her success, even though she came in between theirs.

"My apologies. Where are my manners? I haven't even asked you your name."

"No need to apologize. It's Semaj."

"Oh okay. Nice to meet you, Semaj. I noticed you just got in line when you walked up, but you have to go over to the desk to get the script and fill out some paperwork."

"Thanks, but before I go sign up, this casting call doesn't have anything to do with Randy Martin, does it?"

Semaj's inquiry made Monique's antennas go up.

"I hope not, but why do you ask?"

"Oh, it's a long story. Hopefully, if you have time, we can chat after this."

"It would be my pleasure," Monique replied. She couldn't wait to hear what dirt Semaj had on Randy Martin.

As soon as they were done conversing, Semaj stepped out of line to go get the application and script. As she turned around to walk back, Semaj spotted a few people in line behind Monique who she knew.

"What's up y'all? What took you so long?" Semaj asked, speaking to her business associates, Nicole and Tracy.

"What's up, girl? I see you wanna be like me and be where all the money is," Nicole said.

"And you know this," Semaj answered with confidence.

"Who's behind this one? It better not be that snake Randy," Tamia said, chiming in.

Her question caught the attention of Monique. Suddenly, she started to believe she hadn't been the only one preyed upon after all. Before Monique could turn around and inquire, Semaj introduced her.

"Hey guys, I would like for y'all to meet someone," Semaj said as she tapped Monique on the shoulder for her to turn around.

Excited, Tracy and Nicole placed their right hands over their mouths, and in unison, they said, "Oh my God, Monique Wright!"

"I'm such a huge fan of yours," Tracy expressed.

"Thank you, Tracy. I'm sorry. I don't mean to change the subject, but I couldn't help overhear you bring up Randy Martin's name."

"Oh yeah, girl. He's one of the biggest slimeballs in the business. I can tell you all about him, believe me. We can save that for later, though. Right now, we're here for business."

"You know what? You're right," Monique concurred.

"And while I have your attention, would you like to join us on Facebook. We have a group called Dimepiece, Inc., where actresses network about who's having casting calls and share other business regarding the entertainment industry that can help keep us afloat."

"I don't mind at all," Monique said, feeling that by joining the group she would be able to find out more dirt on Randy. Then she told Nicole and Tracy, "Now, before the two of you get comfortable in line, you have to go over to the table so you can get the script and fill out some papers."

Once the women walked away, Monique turned around to converse with Semaj.

"What's wrong, Semaj? You nervous?" Monique asked, noticing the look of concern written all over her face.

"No, I'm okay. I'm just curious about your inquiries regarding Randy."

Just as Monique was about to tell Semaj, the doors to the ballroom opened and a lady came out and called for Monique, who was up next.

Before walking into the ballroom, Monique told Semaj, "I'll tell you all about what happened after we audition."

Once the doors closed behind Monique, the lady escorted her to the table where the producers for the commercial were sitting.

"Hello, Monique. My name is Greg. Over to my right is Mike and to the left of me is George. We're T.D.A.D, Inc., which stands for Talking Dirty After Dark. We're the newest and latest hotline service, and as you know, you're here to audition for the commercial. We want to capture you two ways: on the couch you see to your right and over by that window. We don't mind if you adlib and add spice to the script you've memorized."

"Thank you. It's nice to meet you, and I'm thankful for the opportunity. Now, where should I start first?"

"Whatever makes you comfortable," Greg replied.

Monique took a deep breath, looked over at the couch, and decided that's where she would start. She even made a quick visualization on whether she would lie across the couch or sit up with her legs crossed while acting out the script. She imagined every girl before her had probably done one or the other, so she decided to do both positions. Monique then got into character and lay across the couch on her stomach. As she stared in the direction of the producers, she started to recite the script in a seductive tone.

"Hello, my name is Monique. Whenever you're bored and need someone to talk to, call me on the Talking Dirty After Dark hotline. Believe me, you wont be disappointed. We can chat about everything. So, while you're thinking about calling, I'll be waiting."

By the time she finished, Monique was sitting up with perfect posture and her right leg crossed over her left.

"Wow, that was nicely put together and the best I've seen today," Greg commented, while Mike and George jotted something down on their notepads.

"Thank you," Monique said, as she mentally prepared herself for the next scene.

"Next up, the window scene," Greg announced, while rubbing his hands together in anticipation of what was about to take place.

Monique slowly walked over to the window and sized up what little space she had for her ass. After making the correct judgment, she sat on the windowsill, crossed her legs, and repeated the script.

Greg applauded along with his partners. "Bravo! Bravo!"

"Thank you for the applause, and again, thank you for the opportunity," Monique told them.

Before leaving the ballroom, Monique walked over to the table and shook hands with each of them. Knowing she had dazzled all three producers, she walked out just like she had entered, full of confidence, only to find that Semaj, Nicole, and Tracy were nowhere to be found. She walked over to the registration table to inquire about their whereabouts.

"Oh my, those three ladies rushed out of here about five minutes ago," the lady informed her.

Just then, she heard the voice of the culprit responsible for the young ladies leaving so suddenly.

"Look at that body. Still in the same shape as when I last saw it."

Monique's body cringed at the sound of Randy Martin's voice. He stood a few feet away drying his hand with a paper towel, and the sunglasses he wore made him look even more like a pervert. Monique thanked the lady at the desk and then approached Randy as he threw the paper towel into a nearby trashcan.

"Maybe you should trade places with that paper towel."

"Awww, you're still down from what took place between us? My apology didn't mean anything to you?" he responded sarcastically.

Monique exhaled as her anger went from zero to sixty in less than five seconds.

"I don't even know why I'm wasting my breath," she said. "I got some important people to catch up with, so get out of my way."

Before Monique could walk pass, Randy grabbed her arm. Monique quickly yanked it away.

"I'm not trying to make a scene, so please leave me the fuck alone," she said through gritted teeth.

"Look, baby, there's no need to go there. But, before you go, I'm working on something new, and it's perfect for you. So, let's bury the hatchet."

"Please! Never in a million years would I consider working for you," Monique said, then walked off.

All she could think about was catching up to Semaj, Nicole, and Tracy. But, by the time she made it outside, they were gone.

Chapter 4

Anxious to connect with Semaj and the rest of DimePiece, Inc. online, Monique drove ninety miles per hour all the way home. She felt her story had to be brought to light ASAP.

As soon as she walked in the house, she got a glass of water, flipped open her laptop, and logged on to Facebook. When she typed in DimePiece, Inc., the link to the group's page popped up, and she clicked on it to request permission to join. While browsing the page, she could see postings from Semaj, Nicole, Tracy, and a couple other females about an upcoming networking party. She sent all three ladies a friend request, and in less than five minutes, they accepted her. Her request to join the group was approved, as well.

Once added, Monique decided it was time to air out her business. She sent them a message, providing all the details about what happened that night with Randy Martin. She also left her phone number so they could call her after reading it. Five minutes later, she received a text from Semaj saying she wanted everyone to meet at Starbucks on City Line Avenue.

Without hesitation, Monique logged off Facebook, grabbed her purse and keys, and hurried out the door.

* * * * *

Upon entering Starbucks, Monique looked to her left and saw Semaj seated in the corner. Semaj greeted her with a hug before they both sat down.

"Where's Nicole and Tracy?" Monique asked.

"Oh, they'll be here. As you saw earlier, those two are always running a little late. So how are you holding up?"

"I'm hanging, but it's like now I ask myself do I wanna know why or should I just leave it all behind and move on."

"Well, let me tell you, I used to date Randy Martin. That was until I caught him fucking Nicole one day."

"Are you serious? How are the two of you able to be friends after the whole ordeal?"

"I put all that bullshit to the side once I found out how conniving the sonofabitch is. Besides, my beef wasn't with Nicole; it was with Randy. DimePiece, Inc. is my company, and I signed Nicole. Everybody tried to warn me to leave him alone, but of course, being young and hardheaded, I didn't listen. Dating him, though, landed me a couple modeling gigs and commercial parts. Before that happened with Nicole, he promised me role in a project, but we broke up right after, and come to find out he ended up giving the part to some girl named Erica."

"Wait! Erica? Erica Banks?"

"Yeah. Do you know her?" Semaj asked.

"I don't know her personally, but I know she has the lead part in *Diva*, a part I was going to audition for."

"Seems like he's fucked over all of us for her."

"Are you thinking what I'm thinking, Semaj?" Monique asked.

Semaj grew quiet and stared out the window for a minute before saying, "About what? Going to find her, whoop her ass, and then cut off his dick?"

"Damn, girl, I ain't trying to go to jail," Monique replied jokingly.

As they were conversing, Nicole and Tracy walked in.

"Sorry y'all. Boyfriend trouble," Nicole said, as she rolled her eyes.

"Yeah, same here. Insecure niggas, I tell you," Tracy added.

"So it looks like we have two thorns in our heels, ladies, and their names are Randy Martin and Erica Banks."

"Oh, the bitch that got my part after I gave him some ass for it? Just bringing up that old news pisses me off," Tracy said.

"I know it does, but the buck stops here with us," Semaj told her. "Randy fucked over the wrong ones. That's why Monique and I are going to come up with a plan to get the truth."

"Yeah, I'm down for the cause, but what do you have in mind, Semaj?" Monique asked.

"Get the bastard alone and then cut off his penis."

Everybody laughed at Semaj's obsession with cutting of his penis.

"I'm thinking it should be done more classy," Monique suggested. "I just want to make him suffer a little and find out the story behind him and this chick."

"So what do you have in mind, Monique?" Nicole asked.

"Nothing at this moment, but I think if we all put our heads together, we can come up with something clever that doesn't involve cutting off penises."

Everybody laughed again. They were laughing so hard that a couple of customers looked over in their direction.

"I mean, we wouldn't have to cut it off, but at least put a blade on the tip to scare him a little," Semaj said, trying to justify her sinister plan. She even acted it while conversing, causing them to laugh at her even more.

"Girl, you're crazy. Monique, I love the idea, but how are we supposed to get him alone?" Tracy asked.

"I'm glad you asked. I ran into him outside of the ballroom right after I finished auditioning. He told me that he has something new for me to look at, so I can use that as bait right there. All we have to do is lure him into a secure location and make him squeal."

"And I want to be right there to see that faggot squeal," Nicole added, becoming sinister like Semaj.

"All of us can be there. That would make it even more interesting. All the women he fucked over in one room. We can call this Operation Vendetta," Monique said.

Semaj smiled hard like The Grinch. "I like the sound of that."

"It's going to take a little planning, so I say we do it the day after the networking party," Monique suggested.

Everybody agreed with Monique's timing.

"Yeah, 'cause I know that prick is gonna show up with his drag queen. I would say let's put the pressure on them there, but we could up end up getting blackballed. So, I can wait until we get him alone," Semaj said.

"I can acknowledge to him there that I want to bury the hatchet and work with him again," Monique added.

"Oooh, I can't wait to see his face when it all goes down. I just love the element of surprise," Semaj stated, while showing off her evil grin again.

Chapter 5

It was the night of the networking party, and Monique along with the other members of The DimePiece, Inc. were gathered at her house, sipping Chardonnay and snacking on cheese and crackers. The main reason they were congregating before the party was so they could discuss their plans for that evening and the next day concerning Randy Martin. Their minds gelled together and formed the perfect plan. However, for it to be official, Monique would have to persuade him that she had forgiven him and wanted to meet with him to discuss the work he had for her. Monique knew she had to pull off the greatest acting in her career. It was crunch time, and not the time to crack under pressure.

Semaj noticed Monique was a little nervous and already on her third glass of wine.

"I see that's your third glass. That's it for you. We need for you to be on point. No mistakes allowed tonight."

"Okay, okay," Monique said, then guzzled down the rest. "I'm not even gonna lie. I'm a little nervous."

"No need to be nervous. Once tonight goes down, we're going to have him right where we want him," Semaj assured her.

"Yeah, Monique, treat this as if you're auditioning for the role of a lifetime," Nicole added.

"So what time does the networking party start?" Monique asked.

"Six o'clock. So, I suggest we get there between seven and eight," Semaj answered.

"Cool. It's five o'clock now, so that gives me more than enough time to sober up and get focused."

Monique's phone started to ring. She looked at the screen and shook her head, knowing what to expect when she answered.

"Hey, Mom."

"Don't 'hey Mom' me. What happened to keeping me informed about what's going on?"

"My bad, Mom. I've been busy lately."

"Yeah, I see. Why wasn't I invited to the party?" her mother asked, hearing the chatter and music in the background.

"It's not a party. I just decided to have a couple of friends over before we head to this networking party."

"Oh okay. Now what did you find out about Ms. Anonymous?"

"Well, she's not anonymous any more, but that's all I can tell you right now. Look, Mom, you caught me at bad time because we're about to leave soon, but I promise I will call you back."

"Okay, and don't forget. I don't want to have to hunt you down again. I would like to know what's going on, too."

"I know you do, Mom. That's why you'll be the first person I call."

After they hung up, Monique said, "Sheesh, that lady can be so relentless at times."

Semaj chuckled, thinking about how her mother was the same way when she wanted to know something.

"Why didn't you just let her know we are planning to hog tie a man and cut off his penis?" Semaj said, adding humor to the situation.

Nicole and Tracy laughed at Semaj's joke, even though they knew she was serious about wanting to do just that. While they were laughing, it dawned on Monique about a certain item in her mother's possession that could be useful.

"Hey, you guys, we have to make a pit stop before we go to the party."

"Where are we going?" Semaj asked.

"My mom's crib. I wanna use some of her makeup for tonight. Matter of fact, we should leave now since it's almost six o'clock."

Everyone grabbed their belongings and headed out the door.

* * * * *

Monique pulled up to her parents' house with the rest of the gang in tow. Before they pulled up, she had called her mother and told her that she was coming to pick up some of her makeup. Monique hopped out and entered the house. As she entered, she interrupted her dad watching TV by giving him a hug and kiss on the cheek.

"Where's ya clothes, Monique?" he asked after receiving her daughterly affection.

"First off, I'm grown, Dad, and second, these are clothes."

"Clothes for what, standing on the corner?"

"Please leave her alone. She's accomplished enough to have her own identity," her mother said, putting in her two cents. "Just remember what your doctor said. You're supposed to be thinking happy thoughts to help your situation."

"Mom! I'm glad I'm only going to be here for a couple of minutes," Monique said before going upstairs.

Once in her parents' bedroom, Monique was unable to find what she was looking for.

"Mom, where's ya purse with all ya makeup inside?" Monique yelled from upstairs.

"It's down here on the kitchen table."

Monique came back downstairs, went into the kitchen, and began the scavenger hunt inside her mother's purse. When she came across what she really came for, she put it in her purse along with a couple makeup items she grabbed.

After saying her goodbyes and I love you's, Monique left ready to paint the town red with her entourage.

* * * * *

When they entered Ms. Tootsies, they had heads turning. Even the men with dates, girlfriends, and wives couldn't help but to stare in their direction. They made it over to the coat check area and checked their purses one by one respectively, but not before taking out their clutches. Then they made their way to the third floor where the party was being held.

Upon making it to the top floor, they witnessed people heavily networking, passing out business cards and flyers to promote their business. They decided not to jump right in, though. They wanted to get a drink first, so they headed over to the bar.

"Hey, guys, I got this round. What do you want to drink?" Monique asked, while pulling out a hundred-dollar bill.

All three ladies ordered the same drink, Cosmopolitans mixed with Ciroc.

After receiving their drinks, they found a spot to sit and look out for Randy. While they sat waiting, they were approached by a couple of modeling agents and producers. They began to grow impatient as time passed and Randy was nowhere in sight.

Nicole and Tracy decided to walk over to the complimentary buffet and get something to eat. They returned with some wing dings, broccoli, and macaroni and cheese, but while gone, they also found out there was a V.I.P. section.

Figuring Randy might be in that area, Monique and Semaj decided to peep inside. There were a lot of people taking pictures with their iPhones and professional photographers snapping photos of a man and woman. After the crowd dispersed, they noticed it was Randy and Erica.

Monique and Semaj quickly walked back to the section where Nicole and Tracy were sitting stuffing their faces.

"They're here. They're here," Semaj repeated.

"Do you think I should approach him while she's standing there?" Monique asked.

"Yes. Fuck that bitch, Mo. If she comes out the side of her face, smack the shit out of her," Semaj said, not afraid of confrontation.

Monique took Semaj's word and walked inside V.I.P. While she was walking in, Erica was walking out. They walked right pass each other, but due to it being crowded in the room, they were unseen by each other. By the time Monique approached Randy, he had already gotten his slimy hands on a young, ambitious P.Y.T.

"Yeah, baby, of course I can make you rich and famous. Here's my card."

"I don't mean to intervene, but can I borrow this man for a moment?" Monique said, while grabbing Randy's arm.

"I see you're doing some fresh recruiting," Monique said sarcastically.

"Ms. Wright, I'm too high for you to bring me down with your sarcasm. You see these people? They came here to see me."

"Oh God! I didn't come over here to listen to you boast about all this. I just wanted to let you know I thought about your offer, and I want to take it."

"Oh yeah? Well, name the place and time, and we can do business."

"I was hoping you could make it the same time and same place as before, and it could be just me and you," Monique replied seductively in his ear.

Monique's words were music to Randy's ears, especially with the affects of the champagne he was sipping on.

"Let's make it tomorrow then."

Perfect, Monique thought as she leaned closer to him.

"That works for me. Eight o'clock, Stage 3, and don't be late."

"Oh, I won't," Randy said, while popping another bottle of Rosé.

"Who let this loser in the winners section?" Erica said as she walked up, staggering from the glasses of champagne she had consumed.

"Loser? Bitch, you better watch ya tone and choice of words," Monique responded aggressively.

"Whaaatever! Randy, who's this groupie, and could you please get her escorted out of here?"

Just as Monique was about to have her palm get acquainted with Erica's face, Mike, the producer from Talking Dirty After Dark, saved her.

"She's no groupie. She's going to be in the commercial along with you. That's right. You two are going to be the faces of T.D.A.D. Talking Dirty After Dark, baby!" Mike said, speaking through a heavy buzz of champagne and doing a stupid dance.

While watching him humiliate himself, the news pierced through Monique's body like one hundred needles. She didn't know how to take it, but knew causing a scene would not be the best thing to do at the moment. So, she played it cool.

"Awww, thank you, Mike, for such good news," Monique said as she hugged him.

"You're welcome, babe." Mike replied with a smile. Turning to focus on Randy he continued... "She absolutely killed the audition. You should think about putting her down with some work, Randy," Mike said, before stepping off in another direction.

Erica boiled with anger. She squinted her eyes and placed her hand on her right hip.

"I don't care who cosigns for you, bitch. You will never be on my level. So, Randy, like I said before, get this flea out of here so the rest of us poodles can mingle."

Monique laughed as if Erica was the lead act for a comedy set.

"Listen, you're not even worth the skin on my palm." Monique's amusement turned cold as she walked closer to Erica. Their noses touched as she continued"But best believe you gonna get yours, bitch."

Monique walked out of V.I.P. and back over to where Semaj, Nicole, and Tracy were sitting.

"So how did it go?" Semaj asked. If she had taken the time to read Monique's body language and facial expression she probably could have answered her own question.

"We good as far as Randy, but get me out of here before I have to kill that bitch."

"Oh my God, what happened?" Nicole asked.

Everybody gathered closer to hear.

"Well, basically, while I was talking to him, she walked up talking shit. She's a bougie bitch that was about to get a serious wake up call. Oh, but I got the part in that commercial, though. One of the producers was in there, and he told me the great news," Monique said, adding some excitement to cut the tension in the air.

After telling them the good news, all three women congratulated her and gave her hugs.

"But, of course, it comes with a catch. It's supposed to be with Erica."

"Oh damn! Are you still gonna do it?" Semaj asked.

"Who knows, but let's get out of here before I mop the floor with that bitch's face," Monique told them.

Everyone agreed to save the celebrating of Monique getting the part in the commercial for another day. Instead, they left so they could prepare for the next day.

Chapter 6

Monique stood in front of Semaj and displayed all the equipment she had purchased at Walmart, which included duct tape, rope, handcuffs...well, the handcuffs were already in her possession, but she included them the other items. She even went out of her way to find a matching white blouse like the one she had worn doing their first encounter.

"I think that's it," Monique said as she put everything back in the bag.

"No, it's not." Semaj pulled out a hunting knife.

"Oh my God! Girl, who you think you are, Crocodile Dundee?" Monique said, getting a hearty laugh from the size of the knife.

Monique was laughing so hard that Semaj ended up joining her.

"You crazy. I'm not really gonna cut his dick off. I just want to scare him with it, that's all."

"I think he's going to piss on himself when you pull that out," Monique said, causing them to laugh again.

"You know what, Monique? After this is over, you're gonna be inducted into The Dimepiece, Inc. as a honorary member. No bullshit, and that's coming from the heart."

"Oh, so you do have a heart hidden behind the maniac in you?" Monique responded jokingly. "Seriously, though, thanks. That means a lot to me. Speaking of Dimepiece, Inc., where are Tracy and Nicole?"

"You should know them two by now. They'll be here any minute. They said they were on their way not too long ago."

Fifteen minutes later, Nicole and Tracy arrived at Monique's house.

"Hey, y'all, what's up? Y'all ready for the real party?" Nicole asked, greeting them.

"Hell yeah!" Semaj said, showing off the knife again.

Tracy walked in as she was showing it off. "Oh my God! We're not going to kill him, are we?"

"No. This is what I call a scare tactic," Semaj told them as she put it away.

"So what's up? Are you guys ready for the show?" Monique asked, talking to Nicole and Tracy.

"Hell yeah, and I want a front row seat," Nicole replied.

"Same here I wanna see him fold in two", Tracy added.

"Well, if that's what the spectators want to see, then I will be sure to put on a good show for y'all. Speaking of show, it won't be much of one without the participator himself. So, let me call and remind him."

Monique pulled out her cell phone and scrolled down until she came to his name. Then she called him and put the phone on speaker so they could all hear him.

"Oh, so you stalking me now?" Randy said when he answered.

Monique stuck her finger into her mouth, signaling how his lameness sickened her.

"Please! I was just calling to confirm our meeting tonight, baby."

"Oh yeah, I'll be there. You just make sure you're ready for me this time."

"Oh, I'm ready, baby," Monique said, then hung up.

"What a lame, y'all. I can't wait to torture this fool. He don't even know what's coming his way."

"That's what puts a smile on my face––the element of surprise," Semaj said, flashing her evil grin.

"So are y'all ready?" Monique asked.

They all agreed that they were.

"Good. Now let me go slip into my outfit and we can be on our way."

* * * * *

Monique and the gang arrived at Jackson Studios a little early to set up. Once they entered, they came across Frank, the security guard, as he was locking down.

"Hello. Which one of you is Monique?"

"I am," Monique replied.

"Well, Randy told me to expect you, but he didn't say anything about you coming with three other people. I will have to clear this with him," Frank said, pulling out his cell phone.

"No, no, Frank. You don't have to call. They are only here to help me set up my stage props."

"Oh okay. Well, after they help, they are going to have to leave, 'cause they are not cleared, only you."

"Sure thing," Monique said with a roll of her eyes. "C'mon, y'all. Forget what he's talking. He's about to leave anyway."

They entered Stage 3, set up the chair, and figured out how to lower the lighting so when on the stage the faces in the audience couldn't be seen. Then they placed the props all around the chair. By the time they finished, it was eight o'clock.

Semaj, Nicole, and Tracy found separate seats respectively, while Monique sat down in the chair on the stage and waited for the arrival of Randy. The sound of the stage doors could be heard closing, and then Randy appeared.

"Oh, I'm gonna enjoy this," he said, noticing the props Monique had lying nearby. "You're going to blindfold me and handcuff me, eh?"

"Whatever you want. Your wish is my command," Monique said seductively, while standing up.

Monique made Randy sit in the chair and mounted his lap. Not wasting any time, he started to caress every inch of her body he could reach, from her breast down to her ass. Monique pretended to enjoy it and begged for more until she got him at the Zenith of excitement. Then she stood up and began to unbutton her blouse.

"So how do you want to start?" Monique asked.

Randy tried to get up, but Monique pushed him back down in the chair.

"I see I'm going to have to tie you up now."

She grabbed the rope and tied him down to the chair.

"Now, let me ask you again. How do you want to start?"

"You on top, please," Randy begged.

Monique walked around the chair and started teasing him by rubbing on his chest. Then she pressed her breasts against the back of his head. Meanwhile, Randy tried to focus on what appeared to be shadows in the seats.

"Do you have people watching?"

"Shut up! I'm the only one authorized to ask questions. Now, because of that, I'm going to have to blindfold you and duct tape your mouth."

After blindfolding him and placing duct tape across his mouth, Randy started to mumble. He was probably cursing her out, but she couldn't care less. Waving, she signaled for the girls to come on stage. Once Randy heard all the footsteps, he began to squirm while still mumbling. After they all were standing in front of him, Monique removed the blindfold and duct tape.

"What the fuck is this?"

"Oh, you're going to find out," Semaj said, being the first to speak.

"Fuck you and ya so-called friends. All four of y'all can suck a dick," Randy said, then spit on the floor in their direction.

Semaj pulled out her knife. "Spit again and see what I do."

"Bitch, you ain't gonna do shit. You don't have the heart to stab me with that."

"Who said this was gonna be used in a stabbing?" Semaj said, gliding the knife around his genital area.

Randy began to sweat and the erection he once had quickly deflated.

"All we want to know is who is this Erica Banks, and how is she connected to you?" Monique asked.

"I'm not telling y'all shit. Y'all gonna have to do more than pull out knives to scare me."

Taking heed to his words, the ladies pulled out lighters and sparked them.

"Hey, what are the lighters for?" Randy asked, growing a little nervous.

"Don't worry. You'll see," Nicole told him.

They let the lighters stay sparked for about two to three minutes while standing there in front of him. Randy sat there wondering about his fate. After letting the metal heat up, they picked a spot and pressed the top of the lighters against his skin.

"AHHHHHH!" Randy yelled from the pain of the heat. "You bitches are crazy! This won't help, though. You can keep burning me. I can take it."

Again, they heated the metal of the lighters and repeated their action.

"AHHHHHHH!" he yelled again.

He tried to wiggle out of the rope, but it was tied too tight.

"Now are you ready to speak?" Monique asked.

"What did I say earlier? I'm not saying shit. My lips are sealed."

Losing her patience, Monique went and grabbed the secret weapon she had brought along.

"Okay, now let's start all over."

"What you gonna do with that taser?"

"If you don't start talking, I'm going to use it," Monique answered.

"Okay, okay! I'll talk. She pays me."

"Pays you to do what?" Monique asked, while walking closer to him with the taser in her hand.

Little did he know the taser wasn't even turned on. She was just using it to scare him.

"She pays me to take roles from people and give them to her."

"So all the roles you gave her she paid you for? Did she also pay you to do the things you did to us?" Semaj asked.

"Huh?" Randy said, trying to play stupid.

"Did she pay you to do the things you did to us?" Monique repeated, raising her voice while pressing the taser against his chin.

Randy panicked, and as he rocked, his momentum caused him to tip the chair over. As he fell onto his side, his cell phone popped out of his pocket. Picking it up, Monique decided to make things interesting and texted Erica to come to the studio. They helped him up, placing his chair in an upright position, but there was no need to finish the interrogation because Randy began to cop a plea.

"Look, I have twenty grand in my office. You guys can have it. Just let me go."

"Twenty grand? I guess Erica gave you that, right?" Monique asked.

"Yes, she did, and now you guys can split that. All I want is my freedom."

"What you think? Should we take the twenty grand and get out of here, or should we torture him some more?" Monique asked, speaking to the rest of the girls.

They came to the conclusion that five grand between them wasn't bad, and let him live. They didn't untie him, though. They left that for Erica to do when she arrived. Randy didn't even know Erica was on her way, but he was excited to see her when she got there.

"What are you doing here?" Randy asked.

"Didn't you text me?" Erica said with a weird facial expression, trying to figure out why he was tied up.

"Don't just look at me! Help me out," Randy demanded.

"Who the hell did this to you?"

"It was Monique and her little Dimepiece Crew."

"Okay, and what did you tell them about me?"

"I didn't say anything. As you can see, they tried to torture me, but I didn't tell them anything."

After she got him out of bondage, they walked into his office, and that fast he had forgotten he gave them the money. He was so busy trying to cover his tracks with Erica that he wasn't thinking correctly.

"Damn, they must have taken my money."

"Okay, let's go find the bitches and get it back."

"Well..."

"Well what? What did you say to them?" Erica said, growing impatient with Randy.

"Well, I haven't been all the way truthful with you. They pulled out a knife and was about to taser me, so I broke down everything."

"You told them everything?! I thought I could trust you." Erica went into her purse and pulled out a nickel-plated revolver.

"Looks like I'll have to fire you, Randy."

Before she was able to pull the trigger, Randy lunged at her, and they began wrestling over the gun. He was able to knock it out of her hands, and the pistol flew across the floor. They were in a tug of war with each other, scrambling to get it. She won by kicking him in the groin area and reaching the gun first. As she turned over, Randy lunged at her, and she fired off two shots, hitting him in the top right side of hischest.

With her adrenaline rushing, Erica jumped up and ran out his office, leaving Randy there to bleed to death.

* * * * *

Monique sat having a breakfast date at her house, reading the *Daily News* with Johan. In between sips of orange juice and bites of eggs, toast, and sausage, she read out loud the details on the infamous Erica Banks.

"You know the people that be writing these captions be dead wrong," she said, laughing at the caption "The Case of When Acting Turns Wrong."

"It sounds like an American Most Wanted case," Johan added, causing them to laugh.

"You're crazy, but it might as well have been. The bitch was crazy. Oh, and get this. Her name wasn't Erica Banks. That was just a name she made up. See, when you got money, you can do shit like that. Her name was Rasheeda Richardson. No wonder she changed her name to Erica Banks. She was a one of them over privileged rich kids that didn't know what to do with herself. See what happens when you are spoon fed? Glad I worked hard for mine."

"All I wanna know is how was it torturing Randy?"

Johan didn't know all the details with Randy assaulting Monique, which was one of the reasons why she did it. She just let him know what she wanted him to know and left out the rest.

"It was wonderful making that fool squeal. Then he gave us five grand apiece. Oh, and now I picked up on some new skills. If you ever try to pull some shit, I got something for you," Monique said, while getting up and sitting in Johan's lap.

As she kissed him, the ringing of her phone disrupted their little intimacy.

"Hey, what's up, Semaj?"

"Nothing. Just calling to see if you got today's paper. Ya girl made the front page."

"Shit, that ain't my girl. Not that crazy bitch."

Semaj laughed. "If it wasn't for Randy surviving, with his lucky ass, she probably would be on the run."

"Yeah, he's definitely lucky. You know what, though, Semaj? I'm glad you called. T.D.A.D. called and told me since your girl Erica is behind bars...oh wait, I mean since *Rasheeda* is behind bars, they have an open spot. They wanted me to help find someone, and you know I thought about you off the top."

"Thanks, Monique. I appreciate that. When do we start shooting the commercial?"

"Tomorrow. I'll call you with all the details later."

After hanging up, Monique turned her attention back to her breakfast date with Johan. She began shaking her head as she thought about Erica being all up in Johan's store.

"You see this picture? I hope you learned your lesson, buddy. Had her all up in ya store, probably all flirting with her. Now look at her. Didn't ya momma teach you to watch out for crazy people?"

After chastising Johan, Monique thought about her mother.

"Oh my God, let me call my mom real quick before she has a heart attack."

As Monique dialed her mother's number, she knew she was going to catch an ear full since her mother had a subscription to the daily paper and probably had already read about the news.

"So you finally decided to call me."

"Yes, Mom. I'm reading the paper and thought about you. Did you get your paper yet?"

"No, I haven't gone outside to pick it up."

"Well, good. Now I can tell all about what happened. You busy?"

"No, I'm not."

"Great, 'cause it's a long story."

Other Great Titles from Johnson Publications:

Emotional Ties-*Jewelze*

Homicide City-*T. Real*

Blue Mirage-*STAR*

Inside Out-*Lati`a D. Johnson*

Inside Out the Aftermath- *Lati`a D. Johnson*

Inside Out 360- *Lati`a D. Johnson*

Scribes In Stilettos *Kia Rogers, Shakina Lewis, Lati`a D. Johnson*

Love Notes To My Father-*Diashon Johnson*

Slipping in Sin-*Sarah Jamison*

Echoes From Heaven-*Sarah Jamison*

Coming Soon...

Cocktales- *STAR, Jewelze, T. Real*

Published- *Lati`a D. Johnson*

Savage- *Lati`a D. Johnson*

Get to Know Us...
www.JohnsonPublicationsBooks.com

www.ingramcontent.com/pod-product-compliance
Lightning Source LLC
Chambersburg PA
CBHW020616250626
47154CB00004B/1538